FOREVER
Young

A PREQUEL
THE TEMPTATION SERIES

ANNIE CHARME

A catalogue record of this book is available from The British Library

This is a work of fiction. Names, characters, organisations, places, events, and incidents are either products of the author's imagination or are used fictitiously.

First Published in 2022 by Chambre Rose Publishing

Forever Young. The Temptation Series. A prequel

PRINT ISBN: 978-1-7399906-1-9

Cover Designed by: Annie Charme

Formatted by: Chamber Rose Publishing

This book is written by a British author. Therefore all spellings and grammar are British English.

Annie Charme on Spotify

Every girl has a best friend, a partner,
and a one true love…
but you're really lucky
if they are all the same person.

CHAPTER One

I walk through the door into the halls of residence, an old building that could use a lick of paint. "You'll only have to share for a while, until a single room becomes available," Mum says, clicking her heels as we walk down the corridor. My steps follow hers and I scan each door, wondering where Cal's room is. *Stop wanting someone unattainable. Mr Right could be right around the corner.* My subconscious tells me. But Cal is Mr Right for me in every way. I just can't have him.

"This is the one." Standing in front of a red door, I take a deep breath and pull down the handle to my student accommodation.

A blonde girl turns around, swishing her long hair, and gives me a warm, welcoming smile. "Hi, I'm Amy."

My brother barges past me, dropping my holdall on the floor, and extends his hand. "Hi, I'm Sebastian."

I roll my eyes at Mum, who just smiles. My brother is two years older than me, studying Engineering in London, so why he is throwing himself at my roommate, I'll never know. Understanding the male brain is a science in itself.

Amy bats her eyelashes at him. "Nice to meet you, Sebastian."

"Call me Seb." He gives her a wink and a grin that makes me want to barf.

"And call me Steph." I butt in, introducing myself.

"Hi, Steph." She stares at the two of us for a beat too long. Her neat eyebrows pull together, painting a quizzical look on her face.

I put her out of her misery. "This is my brother." I can't blame her for wondering. We don't look alike.

Her smile returns. "Oh."

"And my parents." I wave a hand behind me towards Mum and Dad.

"Hi, Amy." Mum steps in front of me and gives Amy a hug and an air kiss on each cheek. "What are you studying, dear?"

"Marketing," Amy replies.

"Me too." My eyes widen and I beam at her.

Mum claps her hands together. "Oh, that's perfect. You two girls are going to have a great time living here. I can see it now, sitting here in your room studying together."

Right? I don't plan on sitting up in my room studying much. And judging by Amy's half smile, I don't think she does either. Let's be honest, I don't think anybody actually comes to uni to study. The fact that we get a degree at the end of it is just a bonus.

"Yes." A half laugh, half huff, leaves my lips.

Dad steps forward with a large container. "Where do you want this, Steph?"

I glance around the room. Amy has already claimed

the left side. "Erm, just pop it on my bed." We each have a wardrobe and a set of drawers and there's a long desk with two chairs positioned under the window.

"Do you want us to help you unpack?"

"No, thanks Mum, I haven't got that much stuff."

"You brought half the soddin' house, Steph." Seb didn't stop going on about the amount of stuff I packed into the car on the journey here.

"I'll get the rest of your things." Dad walks out of the room and Seb follows.

"Where are you from, Amy?" Mum is a nosey sod, wanting to gather as much information as she can about my new roommate.

"I'm from Newcastle." As if Mum didn't already know that, anyone can tell a Geordie accent a mile off. Amy seems nice enough, wearing denim shorts and a t-shirt, nothing too tight or revealing for my conservative mother. However, I would love to have seen my mum's face had I been sharing a room with someone alternative; purple hair, piercings and tattoos.

She hated the company I kept at school, especially my best friend, Callum. 'He's a wrong 'un' she would say. When I told her he was coming to York University, she wasn't impressed. I think she was hoping I wouldn't see him anymore when he moved to the city after our A-levels. Maybe I wouldn't have seen much of him had he not been accepted into the marketing course at York. I haven't seen him since July. Even though we have texted occasionally, we haven't talked as much as we used to, since he started seeing his girlfriend, racy Stacey, a few months ago.

"What about you?" Amy asks.

I fold my clothes up in the drawers. "I'm from a small town in Nottinghamshire."

Mum takes my clothes from the drawer and hangs them in the wardrobe. "When did you get here, dear?"

"Only this morning. I've just finished unpacking and my parents have just left, actually. I was going to have a walk around and get my bearings and maybe check out the student bar."

Now she's talking. "Sounds good. I'll join you. I can always unpack my stuff later."

Dad and Seb return with the rest of my bags and another box, placing them on the bed.

Mum continues to fuss with my clothes. I swat her away. "Mum, stop fussing. I don't need to hang my jeans up."

She tuts and turns to my Dad. "Is that the last of it?"

"Yes, that's all of it. Shall we get some lunch?"

My brother rubs his stomach. "I'm famished."

"We'll stop for food at the services on the way home. We need to get back for Samantha's music performance tonight." My sister, the perfect child, only sixteen and has already excelled at ballet and now plays the violin. There's no end to her talents. I always hoped she would rebel in her teenage years just to make me look good, but she continues to be the voice for the school council and sticks her fingers in any other pies she can get her hands on.

Mum hugs me tight. "Call me on Monday and let me know how your first day goes." Her eyes are glossing over and there is a waver in her voice.

"Okay, Mum. Don't worry." I don't know why she's so emotional. I'm only a few hours' drive away.

Dad hugs me next, giving me his speech that he's been spouting all summer. "Make sure you're safe and sensible. And if you need anything just call me."

"I will, Dad. You know me, always sensible." *Not.*

My brother stands with his hands in his pockets. "Don't do anything I wouldn't do."

"Whatever." I wave them off. My brother's never been one for hugs, unless it involves a hot blonde.

He smiles as they all walk out the door, leaving me alone for the first time in my life, and my shoulders tense. I don't even know how to cook.

Amy grabs a denim jacket. "Shall we have a look around, then?"

"Yes, I can't wait." I pull out my new Nokia and think about texting Callum, but then tuck it back in my pocket. I'm sure I'll see him Monday in class. He's probably busy settling into his room wherever that is.

Amy locks our door behind us. "Your brother is hot."

"He knows it, too." I giggle and shake my head. All my friends fancy Seb. He works out a lot. He's the only person I know that loves to exercise—the freak. His buff body makes up for the fact that he's a ginger. Though, the girls seem to like his freckles and carrot hair for some bizarre reason. I'm just glad I didn't get the ginger gene. My hair is a dark auburn, although I'm blessed with the fat gene—not sure which is the lesser of the two evils? We have our grandparents to thank for that. My granddad is ginger and my grandma is a large woman with a larger-than-life personality to match.

Amy grins with a hopeful glint in her silvery-blue eyes. "Is he at York?"

"He's at London. He has one year left."

"Shame." She points to the student bar across the road.

We walk into the old building full of young people. The din of natters overpowers the music in the background. A long bar lines the wall to the left of the room, and I order half a pint of cider. I follow Amy towards two pool tables in the back and sip on my sparkling apple drink.

Amy sucks her cheeky Vimto with a straw. "I hope we have some hot tottie on our marketing course."

"Mmm. Always good to have a bit of eye candy in class." As I say the words, two arms wrap around my waist, and I get a hot breath in my ear.

"Steph."

I know that voice. I turn around and throw my arms around Cal. "I was gonna text you later."

His soft unshaven jaw rubs against my cheek. "When did you get here?"

I let go of his neck and step back to get a good look at him. I haven't seen him in two months. "Just now. How about you?"

"I came yesterday as my mum had to work today. I told her I could get on the train, but she wanted to drop me off. You know what she's like."

I tuck a loose raven wave behind his ear. "Your hair's grown."

He smiles. "Yeah, I was gonna get it cut, but I decided to grow it out."

"I like it." He's always had long hair that sort of flopped in front of his eyes and he would run his fingers through it and style it back, but now it's much longer, coming to just above his jaw.

Amy coughs. I'd forgotten she was here.

"Cal, this is my roommate, Amy. She's on the marketing course as well."

"Hey." He nods at her, not letting go of my waist.

"Hi, Cal. So you're on the same course as me and Steph?" She twirls the straw around in her purple drink.

Cal's eyes rest on me. "Yeah. Have you met anyone else on the course yet?"

I shake my head. "Not yet."

He taps my hip. "I'm gonna get a drink. I'll tell the lads to come over."

"Lads?" Amy's eyes light up.

"Yeah, a couple of guys who are in my halls. Mark and another lad called Scott. They're at the bar. Back in a minute."

He walks off and Amy leans in. "Steph, I thought your brother was hot but your boyfriend is on fire."

I almost choke on my drink. "Cal isn't my boyfriend."

"He isn't?" She squeezes her eyebrows together and tilts her head to the side. "You looked pretty comfortable to me."

"We're just friends. I've known him practically my whole life."

"Oh, I must say, I thought it odd." She twirls her straw again, rattling the ice cubes against the glass.

I flinch my head back. "What do you mean?"

She shrugs a shoulder. "You just look like an odd couple. You're dressed like you're going to church in your cute lemon dress, and he looks like a demon with his Black Sabbath tee, ripped jeans, eyebrow piercing and all."

I press my lips together and glance down at my outfit. "I don't normally dress like this. My mum picked my outfit this morning, and I thought I would indulge her for one last time."

Do we really look that odd? Not that it matters. He would never go for me. I'm not his type. Most girls at school fancied him, even with his alternative style, he could have his pick. Why would he choose me? I'm nothing special; overweight, dimply thighs, and a podgy stomach. Not that I have a problem getting dates. Granted, the boys I've dated have turned out to be losers, but I've had just about as many guys as he's had girls, which is probably another reason he won't want me. I may look dressed for church, but I'm no virgin Mary.

"So, if he's not your boyfriend, would you mind if I got to know him?"

I don't know how I would feel about that. It would be a bit weird having him date my roommate, but who am I to stop them? "He has a girlfriend. Well, at least he did the last time I spoke to him."

Cal returns with a pint of beer and two lads as promised. Amy puffs her chest out as they come over, making me smile. I think I'm gonna have a lot of fun with her.

Cal waves a hand between the two of us. "Hey, this is my friend Steph, and her roommate Amy."

"Hi, girls," they both speak in unison.

"This is Mark." Cal pats Mark on the back.

He sweeps his straight, brown hair is to the side, out of his steely grey eyes. His smile widens. "Hello." His posh accent doesn't match with his scruffy jeans and Dr Martens. He rolls the sleeves of his checked shirt up to his elbows, while eyeing me the whole time.

"And this is Scott." Cal waves his hand towards Scott, who's already eyeing up Amy's smile. Scott is much neater; short blonde hair with a white t-shirt and dark jeans.

I wave my hand at Scott. "Nice to meet you. What are you guys studying?"

"Scott's on the marketing course with us." Cal takes a swig of his pint.

"And I'm doing fine art," Mark says.

My eyes go wide. "I love art."

Mark steps closer. "Do you paint?"

"No, but I love art history." I smile and his smoky coloured eyes shine as if smiling back at me.

Cal huffs. "Yeah, she's into all that shit."

My eyes roll. "I've signed up for the art history classes. I assume you'll be there too, Mark?"

Mark nods. "It's all part of the fine art course."

Cal stands up straight. "When did you sign up for those?"

I shrug my shoulders, not really remembering when exactly. "Ages ago. I told you."

"Right." Cal looks up, his finger and thumb tug on his eyebrow piercing.

Mark steps in front of Cal. "What artists are you into, Steph?"

"I like all the greats from the Renaissance period. But I also love the more recent modern art too, like Andy Warhol, Roy Lichtenstein, and that whole comic style art." I have to stop and take a breath. I could go on forever talking about this subject.

Mark nods. His eyes are bright like a silvery moon. "I like Surrealism."

I suck in a breath. "Me too. I love Dali. What sort of style do you paint?"

Mark runs his fingers through his hair, moving it to the side so I can get a better view of his lunar eyes. "My style is abstract with lots of bold colour."

"I'd love to come and look at your work."

"Yeah, I bet you would." Cal huffs, before taking another gulp of his pint.

Amy and Scott have their own conversation flowing, and I think Cal's feeling like the third wheel. I squint my eyes at him for being grumpy and then move closer to him, so not to leave him out. "Are you still seeing your girlfriend, Cal?"

He leans against the wall with his foot resting on the brick. "Yeah, why?"

I shrug. "Just asking. I haven't seen you in so long, I'm not sure what you've been up to."

Cal stands up straight. "I texted you last week."

I roll my eyes. "Oh my gosh, Cal. I texted you saying, *'Are you ready for uni?'* And you replied, *'Yes.'* I would hardly call that texting."

He titters, and I glare at him with a hint of a smile playing on my lips.

Mark moves between the two of us again. "Is your girlfriend at York, Cal?"

"Stacey's at Lincoln. She's studying permanent makeup or some shit."

I tilt my head. "Like tattooing your lips and eyebrows and stuff?"

"Fuck knows, I don't know." Cal shrugs his shoulders and lets out a small laugh before taking another gulp of his drink.

Does he even listen to her when she's talking? "When are you seeing her again?"

"I'm not sure. I'll call her this week."

That is so typical of him to put in minimum effort. I met her once. She's lovely and alternative like Cal. She had a Morticia vibe going on with black lipstick and bright red eyeshadow. "What else have you been up to?"

"Not much. I've hardly seen anyone since Mum moved us to the city. What about you? You seeing anyone?"

"No. I didn't see the point in getting serious with anyone, knowing I was coming here." Not that I got any offers, either. There's only one person I'd want anyway, and he's oblivious.

He nods and takes another drink of his pint.

CHAPTER *Two*

A my and I get up early, shower, and dress for our first class. I'm so happy that she's doing the same course as me. It's nice to have a friend to talk to about coursework. I know I have Cal but I don't live with him; he's over in east block. I didn't see him yesterday, either. I spent the day recovering from too many ciders the night before and then unpacked my things.

Amy nudges my elbow. "Are you looking forward to seeing Mark again?"

I smile, thinking of Mark. I do like him. He has that grungy art student look I seem to go for. Not as attractive as Cal, though; that boy has it all going on. I shake the thought, knowing we'll never be anything more than friends, however much I fantasise about him.

I stand in front of the mirror, curling my long hair. "Do you think he likes me?"

"Of course he does. He didn't stop talking to you all night. Even when Cal went to talk to that group of girls, he stayed with you."

I press my lips together when she mentions Cal. "What about you and Scott?"

She giggles. "I'm a little nervous about seeing him again. I actually like him."

"He seemed to like you, too. I mean, why wouldn't he? Look at you."

"Steph, you really think so?" She tosses her long blonde hair over her shoulder and pouts at her reflection in the mirror while putting on her lip gloss.

I grab my bag. "Yep. You ready to go?"

She nods, and we walk out the door.

We arrive at our class and find a table. A group of boys, wearing baggy jeans and ball caps, are already here, and whistle as Amy walks in. She ignores them, and I try not to look their way in fear of drawing their attention to me.

"So immature." She flicks her hair and sits down.

I agree and sit next to her, although I always appreciate the compliment.

Cal walks into the room almost in slow motion, like someone from a Levi commercial with his ripped jeans clinging to his thighs. He shrugs his leather jacket off his broad shoulders, making my mouth water. His gaze meets mine, and he smiles as he walks over, eyeing up the empty seat next to me. Scott follows behind him, but I stay fixed on Cal.

"Hi." I exhale a breathy sigh as he sits next to me.

"Hey." Cal hangs his jacket on the back of his seat.

Scott sits in the seat next to him. "Hi, Steph."

"Hi, Scott."

Amy leans forward. "Hi, Scott." She gives him a wave of her fingers, and I'm like piggy in the middle.

Cal leans back in his chair. "What did you get up to yesterday?"

"Nothing. You?" I pull out a pen and notebook.

Cal nods towards my pen. "I'm gonna need one of those. We went to the bar. I thought I'd see you there again."

I bump his shoulder. "Did you miss me?"

"No." He smirks. "Mark did though."

I hand him a purple pen with a rainbow pattern on. "You know, I have a phone for a reason. So do you. There are buttons on there that you press, and they form words. Then you can actually send those words to another phone and guess what? It makes a little noise, and I can read your message. Isn't that amazing? Your phone does so much more than that stupid snake game you play."

"So. What's your point?"

"If you want to hang out, you can ring me or text me and say, *'Hey, I'm at the bar. Are you coming down?'* I'm not a friggin' psychic. I don't know what you're up to."

"Do you want to hang out tonight?" He places the end of my pen between his teeth and I'm like a schoolgirl with butterflies. Each time our knees knock accidentally, it sends another swarm in my stomach.

A smile pushes my cheeks up. "Yes. What do you have in mind?"

"Dunno." He shrugs his shoulders.

A tall, slender man walks into the room carrying a briefcase. "Hello class. My name is Mr Crawford. I'll be your tutor for the next year. You can call me Adrian."

He begins the lesson and hands out several forms

and other class material, and we all have to stand and say something about ourselves. I sink into my seat, knowing my turn will be soon. The heat rises to my cheeks, and my hands sweat. He goes round each table. A few girls go and then the table with the baggy pants gang and then us. Amy stands full of confidence. Flicking her long hair behind her shoulder. "My name is Amy Bennet. I'm from Newcastle, as you can tell by my Geordie accent, and I like to play hockey."

"Excellent. I assume you've signed up for the hockey club, Amy?"

"Yes, I have, sir. I'm meeting them tonight."

"Great stuff. Who's next?"

I look at Callum. My eyes plead with him to go first. He stands. "Hey, I'm Callum Richards, from Nottingham. I kickbox. Well, I did before coming here. I want to travel and see the world, and I enjoy doing things I shouldn't." He smirks.

Adrian swiftly butts in. "Thank you for that, Callum." Adrian looks at me. "Miss, would you like to tell us about yourself?"

Callum squeezes my leg. I place my hand over his on my thigh, and he clings to my fingers as I stand. I don't know if his grasp is reassuring me or making me worse. His skin on mine causes a stirring in my stomach that I can't explain. *That's your breakfast,* my subconscious tells me.

I take in a deep breath. Callum's thumb strokes the back of my hand, making my head light and dizzy. Here goes. "My name is Stephanie Harrington. I'm from Nottinghamshire, and I like…" My mind goes blank.

Cake, my subconscious says. Shut up. You're not helping, you annoying cow. "I like… er… art and books and…" *Chocolate.* Piss off. "And that's it, really." The heat emanates from my face. I must glow like plutonium right now. Sitting back down with a thump as my legs fail, I sink into the seat, hoping it will engulf my body and transport me back to my dorm.

"Thank you, Stephanie. Who's next?"

Cal is still holding my hand and leans over and whispers into my ear, "You all right?" He knows I hate public speaking and drawing any type of attention to myself. I nod and listen as Scott stands up to say his speech.

"I'm Scott from Durham. I like to watch hockey." He looks at Amy and gives her a wink. Smooth. Very smooth. She flashes him that bright smile of hers. Cal smirks at him. His hand is still holding mine, resting on his leg under the table. I don't want him to let go. It's reassuring, but makes my heart beat faster at the same time.

Eventually, he lets go to take some notes, and I wipe my sweaty palm on my jeans.

At break time, we head to the café, which is near our block. Cal turns to me. "You grab a table. I'll get you a coffee?"

"Thank you."

He disappears to the counter. Amy and I take a seat at a large table near the window. "Was he holding your hand in class?" Amy asks.

I nod, remembering how his hand felt holding mine. A warm fuzziness spreads through my core. "Yes, I told you we're friends. He knows I hate speaking in front of people."

"Have you two ever been more than friends?" She gives me a cheeky smile and there's a glint in her eye.

"No, never." *Only in your dreams*. I've thought about that boy more times than I can remember.

A few other students from our class sit with us, and we get to know everyone. One girl, Nicola, has a job interview tonight at a burger joint on the outskirts of town.

I slump back in my chair and sigh. "I need to get a job."

"Come with me. They're wanting to hire several people. Here, call them. I'm sure there'll be a position for you."

She flips open her clamshell phone and scrolls through the numbers in her address book. I tap the number into my phone with a shaky hand and call them. My voice wobbles a little and I stutter, but secure myself an interview and induction at the same time as Nicola.

She claps her hand together and squeals.

I smile. "I don't have a clue where it is."

Cal returns, shuffling on the bench between me and Amy. "Where what is?" He slides a coffee and baby cupcake my way.

My smile pushes my cheeks up, eyeing the chocolate cupcake. "I've just got an interview and orientation thing for a job at Maccy's, but I don't even know where it is." My body tenses at the thought.

"I'll take you. It's about a ten-minute walk from

here. Maybe a twenty-minute walk for you with your short legs." He smiles and knocks my shoulder with his.

"Cheeky git." I roll my eyes at him, but he always teases me in this endearing way of his.

"When is it?"

"Tonight at six." I blow on my coffee before taking a sip.

His head drops and the smile he wore turns to a frown. "We're not hanging out then?"

"I really need a job, Cal. We can hang out before or after. I just don't know how long this induction thing will take."

"I'll walk with you and wait for you."

My heart swells and my shoulders relax a little, knowing he'll be there. "Thank you."

He shrugs like it's no big deal, but it means everything to me.

A KNOCK SOUNDS at the door. Amy opens it and Cal walks into our room. "Ready to go?"

I turn to face the wall, buttoning my navy floral dress; one of my mother's offerings again, but I'm grateful to her for buying me something smart. "One sec."

My dress comes below the knee and has a collar and a belt that ties around the waist. It pairs nicely with my Dr Martens, which are the only footwear I have other than some strappy sandals or trainers.

He pulls in his bottom lip and looks me up and down. "You look nice."

I narrow my eyes at him, knowing his *nice* means I look pious, but I will take it today. I want to get this damn job, even if it is working at a fast-food restaurant. "Okay, I'm ready."

"Let's go then." He leads the way and I walk beside him. He has his hands stuffed in his pockets and chews on his bottom lip.

I fiddle with the strap on my bag as we cross the road. "This is nice, isn't it?"

"What?" Cal glances at me.

"You, me, us being at uni together. I'm really glad you're here, Cal." All the anxiety and tension weighing on my chest seems to disappear when he's close, and I can do anything with him by my side.

"Me too." He nods and smiles.

"Have you called Stacey yet?"

He looks down at the pavement as we walk. "She called me earlier."

"Is she all right?"

"Yeah, she's settled in all right, she's coming over next weekend." He glances sideways at me.

I nod and force a smile. "Cool."

"She asked about you."

My eyes widen. "Really? What did she say?"

"She said we could all go out together if you wanted to. I said we didn't have to go anywhere, but she didn't want to stay in the dorm all night. I told her we could stay in the living area, and I'd tell the lads to clear off for the night."

ANNIE CHARME

"Cal, you can't monopolise the living area."

"They're cool. I told the lads I would return the favour when they want a fuck."

"Cal." I swat his arm.

He titters. "What? I have needs."

I shake my head. "Too much information."

"What, you don't have needs?" He raises an eyebrow at me.

"Not like you, randy sod." Although of course I have needs. I need him more than he'll ever know.

He chuckles to himself.

I see the large sign for the restaurant as we turn the corner. "Are you gonna get a job? Nicola said they're hiring a few people. Why don't you have a word while you're there?"

He jerks his head. "Fuck off. I'm not working there."

I squish my eyebrows together. "Why not?"

"You wouldn't get me wearing one of those fucking hats for a start, or those badges with the shitty stars on."

I press my lips together to stifle my laugh. He's right, I could not picture him there at all. "You could pull off the badge. You could make it look cool, I'm sure."

He narrows his eyes. "I'm never going to find out. Plus, I'm all right for a bit. I don't need a job yet."

"You're lucky you have a government grant."

Cal opens the door to the restaurant. "I applied for a student loan too. Figured I may as well go for it."

"So did I. I'll still be paying that shit off when I'm forty. I'm sure of it."

He chuckles. "Me too. Fuck it."

I walk through the door and look at my watch. "We made it in fifteen minutes."

"Wow, you must have had a spurt on."

I swat his chest. Glancing around, I'm not sure who I need to see or where I need to go, and my stomach tightens.

Cal places his hand on the small of my back and whispers, "Are you all right?"

"I think so." My body temperature rises, but I'm not sure if it's nerves of being here or his hand on my back and his warm breath on my neck.

"Don't be nervous. That bloke there looks like the manager." He points to a man with a tie and a name badge and pushes me forward. "I'll wait here for you."

"Okay." I take in a deep breath, walk towards the tills, and introduce myself. The manager takes me into a back room with four others, including Nicola, who is already here, and we fill out some forms. At the end of the induction I get my rota. I'm thrilled that I've secured a part-time job in my first week. I walk back out to Cal, still sitting at the table sucking a milkshake dry.

"Hi." I sit down next to him with an aching smile on my face.

Cal places his drink on the table. "How did it go?"

"I start on Thursday."

He grabs my arm and gives it a shake. "That's great."

Two empty burger wrappers, a large fries carton and an empty box of nuggets adorn on the table. "Have you eaten without me?"

"Yeah, I couldn't wait any longer. You were in there over a fucking hour."

My tummy grumbles. With everything going on, I hadn't thought about food until now. "I'll grab a burger then."

"Get me one of those ice cream sundaes… and an apple pie."

I roll my eyes and tut as I walk to the till, jealous that he can eat this crap and still have an amazing body.

Returning to the seat with my chicken burger, fries and diet drink, I hand Cal his ice cream and pie. "Here, you greedy pig."

"I'm a growing lad. What can I say?"

I smirk at him and salivate as he licks the ice cream from the spoon. "I appreciate you waiting for me, Cal."

"No worries." He licks the spoon again, and I imagine his tongue licking me, and a tingle pulses through my body.

"I'm looking forward to art history class tomorrow." I bite into my chicken sandwich.

"Is that because of Mark?" He crinkles his forehead.

I furrow my eyebrows. "No, Mark has nothing to do with it."

"If you say so." He shrugs and continues licking the ice cream sundae.

I lean closer to Cal. "Has he said anything about me?"

"No. He asked if I knew where you were yesterday."

I suck in a breath. "What did you say?"

Cal flinches his head back. "I told him I'm not your fucking keeper. Do you fancy him?"

I lean back in my chair and huff. "No."

"Could have fooled me." He titters and mocks in my voice. "Oh Mark, I love art. I love Andy Warhol. I love you."

"Ugh, whatever." I whack his chest with the back of my fist. He mocks me again like I have pierced his heart, rubbing the area over his Motley Crue t-shirt.

I take a sip of my drink. "I need to find out where the lecture theatre is."

"It's down past the café and to the right, behind the pottery block."

"Oh, great. Have you digested a map of York or something, you seem to know where everything is to say you only arrived Friday."

"Yeah." He picks up his apple pie and takes a bite. My mouth waters as the gooey centre drips and he licks his lip. I can almost taste it. "Wanna bite?" he muffles with a mouthful.

I nod, mesmerised by the pie and his lips. Cal brings it to my mouth, and I take the biggest bite I can. "Watch my fingers." Cal chuckles. And I hide the smile as I chew the sickly sweet pastry and the warm apple sauce glides along my palate.

We step out of the restaurant into the setting sun. I wrap my arms around my breasts and rub my arms, fighting off the chill in the air.

"Here, have my jacket." Cal hands me his leather coat. I wonder if I will actually fit in it, although his shoulders are broader than mine, so I give it a go.

"Thanks." It's comfortable, but it won't meet past

my large breasts. Cal smiles as I try to tug the leather past my boobs, but it's no use.

"Your girls getting the nip on?"

"What?" I glance at the two prominent bullets under the fabric of my dress and my cheeks flush.

He laughs and puts his arm around my shoulder as we walk. Then kisses my hair. "I'll warm you up." I suck in a breath. His raspy voice causes a flicker deep inside me. I look up at his unshaven face and scan the short hairs that trail down his neck, and I want to feel his soft stubble against my skin. What's wrong with me? We've been friends for years, but I've never had these feelings for him before. *Liar.* Okay, I've always found him attractive, even in junior school. I've just never allowed myself to think of him as anything other than a friend, but right now I can't stop myself.

Thinking of his girlfriend, I look away—lucky cow. I wonder if he gives her his jacket? Does he hold her hand as gently as he did mine in class today? Does he kiss her hair as tenderly as he kissed mine? I lean into his shoulder as we walk. The breeze blows, and I catch his scent; a fresh salty sea breeze mixed with mint.

"Amy and I are going out this weekend. Why don't you and the lads come out with us?"

"I'll mention it, I'm sure they'll be up for it."

"Cool." The warmth from my cheek spreads through my body, and the smile on my face makes my jaw ache.

CHAPTER Three

After lunch, I say my goodbyes to the girls and head to my art history class. Everyone else has a free period. I remember what Cal said about walking by the café and around the back of the pottery block. The window of the pottery class is filled with amazing sculptures; some abstract contorted figures and some very detailed realistic pieces.

Eventually I come to the lecture theatre building. Entering, I see Mark and decide to make a beeline for him. As I am about to walk down the steps towards his aisle, an arm wraps around my waist, pulling me back.

I suck in a breath and turn around to see Cal smiling. "What are you doing here?"

He shrugs. "I signed up."

Although I'm elated to see him here, I squish my eyebrows together. "You hate art."

"No, I don't."

I frown at him, and he waves a hand, gesturing for me to sit down. Mark is a couple of rows in front and hasn't seen me, but there is no contest, really. I will always choose Cal over another lad. Even if we are only friends, I'm drawn to him. He does things to me I just haven't felt before, and the tingle I get from a graze of his hand or the way he smiles at me is an addiction. My body craves any scraps of affection he throws my way.

I scoot down a few seats, stepping sideways in the rows of folding chairs. Cal follows and sits next to me. I pull out a pen and notebook.

"Do you have a spare pen?"

Typical. "What happened to the last one I lent you?"

"I left it in the other class."

I roll my eyes and pull out my sparkly pencil case, and hand him a pink pen with a smirk. "Here, don't lose it."

He taps it against his lips and then points at Mark in front of us. "Oh look. Your lover boy's here."

I push his hand down, and my eyes widen. "Keep your voice down. Don't call him that."

"Why not? You fancy him. I can tell."

"You don't have a clue who I fancy, Cal."

He whispers in my ear, "I know you better than you know yourself, Stephanie." If that were true, he would know how I feel about him. He tears out a piece of paper from his notebook.

"What are you doing?"

He folds it up to fashion a paper aeroplane and throws it at the back of Mark's head.

"Cal." I knock his leg with my knee.

Mark looks around and casually waves. I smile and wave back, sinking into my seat and looking away. Cal mocks me when Mark turns back to the front. "See, you fancy him. I saw how you waved at him." He re-enacts my shy wave and bats his eyelashes.

"Piss off." I elbow him in the chest, and he mocks me again like I've stabbed him in the heart.

A middle-aged woman appears on the stage. Her hair is silver with a purple undertone and practically glows under the stage lighting. She pushes her spectacles up her nose and tugs at her bobbled cardigan. The lights go dim as the lecturer clears her throat and begins her presentation.

"Today we are going to learn about Beryl Cook. A British artist, born in Surrey and widely known for her paintings of chubby, usually jovial characters."

She flicks the switch on the projector, and we get the first slide. A painting of a bunch of women at what can only be described as an Ann Summers party. A buxom woman is holding up a skimpy red thong, another a red bra, while the others hold a glass of wine. I smile at the slide. Having been to one of these parties with my auntie, it was a bit of an eye opener. I listen intently as the tutor tells us more about the artist.

"Cook's subjects are drawn from everyday life and frequently involve the saucy humour associated with seaside holidays." The next slide is a bunch of larger women in a pool on a cruise ship, followed by a more slender woman in a fur coat with burgandy bobbed hair.

"It's your mother." Cal titters. I let out a snort as I try to hold in my laugh. It does look like my mother in her pretentious attire. The next slide is a bunch of giggly girls on a night out showing off their chubby thighs in short skirts.

"That'll be you and your mates on Friday." He laughs silently, rocking his shoulders against me.

"Piss off and shut up. I'm trying to listen," I whisper yell. But can't help smile with him as I shake my head. "Cheeky twat."

———————

FRIDAY NIGHT COMES AROUND QUICKLY and a group of us are going out around York. It's my first time in the city. Knowing Mark is going, I want to look my best. Of course, I want to look my best for Cal too—I always want to look good for him—even though we'll never be anything more than friends. Amy rifles through my wardrobe and pulls out my black and pink checked skirt that comes halfway up my thigh and a hot pink top that ties at the front.

"Cute," she says when I put it on and do a twirl. I don't want to look cute. I want to look hot, but this is about as good as it gets with my current wardrobe. Now that I no longer have my mother breathing down my neck, I should go shopping.

Amy slips on a slinky purple dress that clings to her perky boobs and bony hips, making her body look absolutely amazing. I stand next to her and look in the mirror, seeing my body next to hers has me tugging my skirt down to hide my dimply thighs. But she's right, I do look cute in this outfit. The other girls rock up at the dorm. "Are you ready?"

I slip on my black sandals, top up my lipstick and shove it in my purse. Amy is smoothing down her long hair.

"I am, let's go." I hold the door for her. Grabbing her purse, she steps into the hallway, and we walk to the main bars lining the high street. The first pub we come to, I spot Cal, Mark, Scott, and a few others at the bar. Cal stands, leaning against the wall in his black attire that looks so good on him.

Mark stands next to him in his usual grungy style; a white t-shirt and jeans with a checked shirt that hangs open. He runs a hand through his straight brown hair when he sees me, sweeping it to the side of his forehead. "Stephanie."

"Hi, Mark."

"What are you drinking?" Mark asks. But before I can reply, Cal shouts to the bartender, "Add a half cider onto that order, mate."

I glare at Cal. "Thanks, but I might not have wanted a cider."

"You always have a cider." He's right, I do, but tonight I wanted to have a girly drink, a cocktail or wine. *Who are you trying to impress?* I don't know, but I didn't want to get bloated with cider. I already feel frumpy in these clothes.

"What did you think of the art history lecture?" Mark asks.

"I really enjoyed it and learnt so much. I'd heard of

Beryl Cook before, but hadn't really studied her. Her work is amazing how she portrays larger characters and depicts scenes from everyday life and pub culture."

"You liked how she painted fat women?" Mark chuckles.

Cal hands me my half a cider. "She painted the average woman."

I smile at his use of words and how he finds the women in her paintings normal, or is he just saying what he knows I like to hear?

Mark nods along, drinking his pint and licking the froth from his upper lip. "I think Marie, the tutor, is looking at that French geezer next week, Toulouse-Lautrec I believe."

"I can't wait."

The other girls join our huddle with their bottles of WKD Blue and cheeky Vimtos. Amy goes straight to Scott. Cal turns to talk to some of the other lads, leaving me to continue talking to Mark.

After we've finished our drinks, we move on to the next bar. The girls and I chip in for a pitcher of strawberry mojito cocktail. Amy pours the drink into my glass and hands me a straw. I must have got the bottom dregs because it tastes quite strong, but I'm not complaining.

"What's that?" Cal asks, but before I say anything, he has taken my straw in his mouth and tried it for himself. "Nice."

"Some strawberry cocktail, I thought you'd like that." I take the straw between my lips, knowing it was just in his mouth, and suck up the sweet fruity liquid, imagining my lips are against his.

In the next bar, Scott orders shots for us all. I take the shot glass and inspect its contents; a clear liquid with gold floaters.

"What the fuck's this?" Callum shouts over the music before knocking it back in one go. He doesn't flinch. Just the smell of this is making my eyes water.

The girls do a countdown. "Three, two, one. Go." I close my eyes and toss it in my mouth. The liquid is like flames licking my tongue, setting my oesophagus on fire as I swallow it down. Cal laughs at my screwed-up face, sticking my tongue out into the cool air, anything to cool down my mouth.

"Goldschlager." Scott shouts over to Cal.

My head shakes. I'm gasping for water. "That was evil." I swat at Cal for laughing so hard.

"Let me get you another. I need to see that face again."

"Piss off. I'm not having another."

As the night goes on, we all end up at a nightclub. Last time I saw Mark, he was with a bunch of his fine art class mates and said he would catch us up. I was sure I would get off with him tonight, but he isn't anywhere to be seen. Amy and Scott are kissing in a booth somewhere. I leave them to it and stand with Nicola and the remaining girls. Cal is here somewhere with some of the lads. I've moved on from my usual cider drink to a cheap wine. I couldn't take any more fizzy alcohol. My stomach is so bloated, although I made a bad choice with the wine as it's gone straight to my head, making me dizzy. Or was it all the alcohol I had before? Whatever, this wine seems to have topped me off. I make a mental note to get water the next time I go to the bar.

Loud music pierces my ears. Nicola shouts over the beat, but nothing she says is sinking in. I'm focused on the darting coloured lights illuminating her face when two hands grab my arse cheeks, bringing me back to the present. My eyes widen, and my first thought is that Mark has decided to make a move. I suck in a breath and my heart picks up a pace as I turn, hoping for a kiss only to see a pisshead slobbering all over me. He leans in for a smooch, pressing his lips to mine and a little bit of sick rises into my mouth. I push him off, and he pulls me back with him, slathering on my neck.

"Get off," I shout and shove him again. He isn't getting the message.

"Oh come on love, you can thank me later." As though I should be grateful or something to have him grope me.

"Sod off, you creep."

"Fuck off then. I didn't wanna fuck a fat cunt, anyway."

I open my mouth and lift my hand, ready to slap him across the face when Cal comes out of nowhere and pummels his fist into his jaw. The dickhead falls back onto a group of people who push him back towards us. Cal punches him in the stomach. He retaliates with windmill arms, but Cal swerves out of his way and grabs hold of his shirt. "Keep your dirty hands to yourself and your fucking mouth shut."

"Fuck you," the drunk says, causing Cal to throw another punch that hits him right in the eye. Some other guy swings for Cal, coming at him from the side and lamps one on his face. Scott jumps into the mix, defending Cal. It's a full on brawl. I'm frozen, watching it all unfold in slow motion. The slobbering fool falls back again and stands on my toe, making me scream and snap out of my transfixed state.

The bouncers wrestle the guys to the floor and drag them out of the club. They restrain Cal's hands behind his back as they escort him out, along with Scott and the other two. I run after them, wincing with my throbbing toe, and Amy follows Scott. My heart races. I need to get to Cal and check he's all right. Once outside, the cool air hits me. I'm not as dizzy as I was a moment ago. Scott walks Callum down the street, away from the other guys, coaxing him down from his fury. I run to them but limp when my foot hurts. There's a throbbing ache emanating from my big toe and when I look down at my strappy sandals, it's covered in blood, matching Callum's cheek.

"Oh my gosh, Cal." I put my hand on his face and inspect his injury.

He flinches, moving his face away from my hand. "I'm good, Steph." His jaw clenches, looking down the street for the idiot that caused all this.

"No, you're not. You have a gash on your cheek. Did he have a ring on or something?" I blink away tears, knowing I caused this.

"Fuck knows, but if I see him again, he's havin' it."

Scott's laughing. Adrenaline has him hyped up and animated. "Fucking hell, Callum. What happened? One minute you're standing there suppin' your pint and the next minute you're pummelling some guy's face in."

"He fucking deserved it." Callum looks at me, and I know he saw and probably heard what that prick said.

"Why, what did he do?" Scott spits on his white t-shirt and rubs at the blood splattered on his sleeve.

"Doesn't matter." Cal places his hand on my cheek. "Are you all right?"

I nod and gulp, choking back a sob.

Scott re-enacts Cal's movements and fists the air like Rocky Balboa. "Fuck, remind me never to cross you."

"Cal's right. He deserved it. He was being a dick." I examine Cal's face some more. "Let's go back to the dorms, get you cleaned up." I also need to sort my foot out. It feels like my toenail is hanging off, but I daren't look.

"We'll come back with you," Amy says.

"It's cool. I'm fine. You can all stop fussing." Cal moves his head away from my hand.

"Do you want to grab a kebab?" Scott asks Amy.

"Sure, I'll see you back at the room later, Steph."

"Okay." I wave my hand as they turn in the opposite direction.

Cal nods towards them. "You can go with them. You don't have to come back with me."

I lock my arm through his. "But I want to come back with you."

He shrugs, and we walk to the halls. My big toe throbs with every step, but I try not to let on. "Where's your room, anyway?"

"I'm on the east block."

I hold on to Cal as we walk, using him as a crutch. "You didn't have to do that, you know."

"Yes, I did. Fucking dick wouldn't take no for an answer." A trickle of blood runs down his cheek over his clenched jaw.

"I could handle it. You didn't have to get your face bust up for me."

He stops in our stride and turns me to face him. "Nobody talks to you like that, Steph. Nobody."

I wrap my arms around his shoulders and pull him close for a hug, making sure my head goes to the side of his face that isn't smeared with blood. His arms slide around my waist, and he kisses my hair. His heart beats at the same rapid pace as mine. It must be the adrenaline.

An overwhelming feeling of love washes over me and I swallow the lump in my throat as my eyes well up again. I'm not sure my own brother would have defended me with as much passion as Cal did. I kiss his neck where my head rests before I pull away, and we continue to walk to the rooms. Cal turns towards the west block.

"Cal, I thought you were on the east side?"

"I am, we're going to your room."

"Oh, okay." I scramble in my purse for my key and realise I've sobered up since the drama. I also left a half full glass of wine in the club too. Good job really, as I think I may have puked had I had any more alcohol, although it may have numbed my toe.

I turn the key in the lock and open the door. "Wait here, I'll get something to clean your face."

Cal sits on my bed and I hike down the hall to the bathroom and return with a wet warm flannel. Cal is topless in my room and laid on my bed with his arms folded above his head. The sight of him gives me a tingle in my core. I perch my bum next to his waist, causing a dip in the mattress as I lean over to wash the blood from his face.

Each time I wipe over the gash on his cheekbone, his eyes flicker, and I can somehow feel the pain there, too. "That idiot has made a right mess of your cheek."

"I'll live." He tucks my curls behind my ear as I wipe his cheek. My face hovers over his, and I want to kiss his cut better.

"I'm sure that drunken prick looks worse though." I smile, wiping the last of the blood from around his cut. It doesn't seem as bad now that it's clean, although it's swelling already, and a purple hue creeps out from the wound onto his pink skin.

"I've had much worse. Don't worry." The corner of his mouth curls upwards, opening the cut again on his cheek.

"I remember when you and Dean got into a fight. You were shitfaced and too wasted to defend yourself."

Cal chuckles. "Good times."

I can laugh about it now, but I wasn't laughing at the time. Neither were they. Cal's fingers graze up and down my arm, leaving a shooting trail of goosebumps in their wake. He lies on his side to make room on the single bed for me and pats the duvet for me to lie next to him. I carefully slip my sandals off and lift my feet onto the bed. My bloodied foot sticks out like a sore thumb. *Toe actually*. Whatever.

Cal sits up. "What the fuck happened to you?"

"That prick stood on my toe when you punched him and he fell onto me."

"Why didn't you say? Pass me that flannel." He wipes my toe. "I wish I'd knocked his fucking teeth out now." His voice is deep and his lips press into a hard line as he breathes heavily through his nostrils, but his hand on my foot is the most gentle of touches.

I sit up and watch Cal clean the blood away. "You will probably be barred from that club, you know."

"Fuck it."

"You can't go beating up every guy that calls me fat." I suck the air in through my teeth as the flannel catches my nail.

"Watch me."

"Cal, I'm serious. People have called me names my whole life. I'm used to it. It doesn't bother me, really."

Even though it does bother me, it hurts each time someone makes a derogatory comment about my weight, and all the backhanded compliments over the years have left scars. 'Oh, you're really pretty for a big girl', 'be thankful you have big boobs.'

"It bothers *me*, Steph. Nobody talks to my girl like that." My girl? My heart flips into a little dance. If only I were his girl; his girlfriend and not just a friend who happens to be a girl.

I wonder if Stacey knows how lucky she is to kiss those perfect lips. To run her hands down his stomach the way I want to now, and unbutton those tight jeans to feel how big he is in my hand and my mouth. Oh, gosh, I'm drooling.

"Is my nail hanging off?"

"No, but it might be black under your pink nail varnish. It's cut down the side, but it's not bleeding anymore."

He lies back down next to me. I lift my head so he can tuck his arm under my neck, and I snuggle against his bare chest. Nothing has ever felt more perfect than right now. His fingers gently twirl my long curls. My breathing is erratic, and my heart is having a party on the vengabus.

"Thank you."

"What for, cleaning your toe?" His chest shakes as he laughs under his breath.

I slap his stomach. "Stop it, you know what for."

"You don't have to thank me. I will always be there for you." He kisses my forehead, and the disco in my heart turns up a notch.

"Cal. You're my best friend, you know that, right?"

"I know, baby." Baby? He hasn't called me that before. The word reverberates over my skin, making the hairs prick up on my arms. Even my nipples stand to attention. We lay on the bed in silence. I close my eyes and imagine I am his girl, and this is how we spend our nights; cosy and snug. His fingers running through my curls, and my fingernails teasing his tight stomach. No awkward silences. We can just be together and not speak. We know each other well enough to be comfortable like this. He's right, he knows me better than I know myself, but he doesn't know my secrets, he doesn't know how much I want him right now.

CHAPTER

O n screen is a portrait of what appears to be a woman being worshipped sexually by several others at the same time.

The tutor walks on stage. "Afternoon, class today we are discussing eroticism in art forms. First up, we have Octave Tassaert's painting Le Femme Damnee, which translates to The Damned woman."

I peer at the image, studying every detail.

Cal leans into me, his breath caressing my neck, causing the hairs to stand to attention as he always does. "Damned? She looks like she's doing pretty well to me." Him in the ribs with my elbow.

Our tutor continues to discuss the piece. "This painting looks more like heaven than damnation; a common fantasy for most people."

He leans in again, his lips brushing my ear. "Is that a fantasy of yours?"

His faint caress against my skin travels to my centre and I have the urge to cross my legs.

"One man is enough for me." It's him. Only him. I don't fantasise about being with anyone else.

He has a smug smile on his face as he leans back in his seat, lifting his hands to rest behind his head.

"Especially as the three people are all women." I smile, sucking the end of my pencil.

"Are they?" His eyebrows pull inwards and he leans forward in his seat to get a better look at the picture on the large projector.

I love it when I know something he doesn't. He thinks he's more intellectual, but with art history, I win every time. "Yes. It's basically saying she's damned for her sexual preference, which clearly was not widely accepted at that time."

He seems to be a little more interested in the class, as he doesn't speak for the rest of the lesson. I have to check he hasn't fallen asleep, as he's unusually quiet. Obviously, art erotica keeps his attention.

CAL SITS across from me with a burger and fries in the campus café. "Stacey's coming to stay for the weekend. You still coming out with us tonight?"

"I don't know, Cal." I smooth my fingers over a lock of my hair that flows in front of my shoulder. The last thing I want is to watch Cal and racy Stacey all pissin' night.

"There's a group of us going out." His eyes are pleading with me to say yes. Normally I wouldn't hesitate to go out, but I'm not sure how much of Stacey I can stomach. The thought of seeing Cal hold her hand and kiss her lips makes my insides twist. I can already taste the acid in my mouth just thinking about the two of them. His gorgeous smile reaches his alluring eyes, and I can't help but please him.

"Okay." I steal one of his chips.

"Do you want some food?"

"I've had a salad."

"Yeah, I know. No wonder you're still hungry. Here, have some." He pushes his plate towards me so I can share his meal.

"Thanks." I take another chip and dip it in his ketchup.

"Scott's coming. I'm sure Amy will be with him and a few others. We're meeting at the Lion pub at eight."

"When does Stacey get here?" I lick my lips as he bites into his burger.

"Wanna bite?" Cal mumbles with a mouthful of food.

My eyes widen, and I nod like a panting dog waiting for a treat. He brings the burger to my mouth and I take a bite. "Mmm." My eyes close, tasting the meat and red sauce.

Cal finishes the rest of his burger and licks his fingers. "Her train arrives in half an hour, so I'm skipping the afternoon classes to meet her."

"I'll come with Amy."

He slides the rest of his chips to me. "Finish them. I'm off." He stands and squeezes my shoulder. "Stacey'll be glad you're coming."

I smile as he walks off, but once he's gone, I screw my face up. *'Oh, Steph, I'm so glad you came'.* I mimic in her voice. *'I'm so glad Cal has you as a friend.'* She knows she doesn't have any competition with me—the fat girl who's friend-zoned. I'm sure Stacey's a nice person. I need to stop being bitter and jealous.

Amy sits down and steals one of Cal's chips. "What's up with you?"

"Hmm?" I glance at Amy.

"You look like a right sour faced sod." She takes another chip.

I sigh. "I'm okay."

"No, you're not. What's got you in a mood?"

I sit up straight and plaster a fake smile on my face, folding my arms across my chest. "Nothing, I'm not in a mood."

She shrugs, dipping the potato chip into the red sauce. "I know what will cheer you up."

I tilt my head and tap my foot. "What?" Please tell me Stacey has the chicken pox and isn't on the train. *You're being a bitch again.* Sod off.

"I'm staying at Scott's tonight so you will have the room to yourself." Her smile reaches her eyes, making them shine like molten silver.

"How is that going to cheer me up?" I huff.

"Because…" She wiggles her eyebrows.

"I'm hardly going to have a good time all on my billy-no-mates, am I?" I cram the remaining chips in my mouth and miserably chew them down.

"I thought Cal could stay over. You two looked pretty cosy when I came back to the room last Friday. Until he left, that is." She pokes my ribs, making me jerk and giggle.

"Until you barged in the room and woke him up,

you mean." I was so comfortable in Cal's arms. I wanted him to stay all night.

"Sorry about that."

"I told you it's fine. I don't think he planned on staying. We just fell asleep." *He fell asleep. You were too busy fantasising about being his girlfriend.* My subconscious corrects me. A girl can dream, right?

"I thought you might want to invite him over tonight. See what happens." She nudges me again with her elbow.

I tut. "Amy, he has a girlfriend."

"His girlfriend's not here, is she? You are." Her finger pokes at my ribs again and it tickles.

I slump down in the chair. "She's coming over. Like now. He's gone to meet her at the train station."

"Oh." Amy leans back and taps her finger against her chin.

"And besides, I've told you we're just friends. I've known him since I was about five years old."

"I can tell you like him, though, right? You can't deny it. I've seen how you go all giddy when he shows up and after he cracked that guy last week, I thought maybe he must have feelings for you too."

"We both care about each other. We've been friends for a long time, but that's all we'll ever be." The air blows upwards from my mouth, lifting my fringe.

"Ok, I'll drop it. What about Mark then? Do you like him?"

"I do, but I don't think he's bothered."

"I'll set you up tonight." She claps her hands together.

"Amy, please don't. If he doesn't like me, I would be so embarrassed."

"I'll ask Scott to do some digging and find out if he likes you." She smiles and we make our way to class.

I GOT PAID TODAY; my first wage from my new job. After class, I walk to the high street, heading straight for my favourite store that caters to my shape. I try on several outfits, eventually settling on a black dress. It's plain but flattering and sexier than anything I own. It's about time I treat myself to a new outfit.

Back at the rooms I make myself a pot noodle. I've been living on these lately and burgers at work. Each time I do a shift, I get a free meal, which is convenient. My cooking skills extend to beans on toast, scrambled eggs or a cheese sandwich.

"Steph, aren't you ready yet? We're going soon." Amy walks into the kitchen to open a bottle of White Lightning with Nicola, getting a head start on the alcohol.

"I went into town after class. Don't worry. I'll be ready; just give me an hour."

"Hurry up. Do you want a glass of this?" She waves a bottle of White Lightning in my face. The clear fizzy drink makes my stomach turn. Last time I had that swill, I threw up. The vomit ran down my friend's scrawny calf, into the gap left by her too loose knee boot. She wasn't impressed. Neither was I. I had to go home and sleep it off, missing out on all the fun.

"No thanks, I can't drink that stuff anymore."

I rush off to get ready, curling my long dark auburn hair and applying my night-time makeup; glittery eyeshadow and pink lipstick. Then re-apply my nail varnish to hide the hideous black nail after getting trodden on by that jerk last week. I wince when I slip my sandals on as the strap catches. Maybe I should have a drink of White Lightning. It may numb the sting in my toe.

Amy pops her head in the room. "Steph, are you ready? We're all waiting for you."

I squirt my fruity perfume that Cal says smells like strawberries. "I'm coming. Keep your knickers on."

"I would, but I'm not wearing any." Amy giggles.

"Amy, seriously?" I look at her skin-tight purple dress that shows off every contour of her body.

"I couldn't wear any in this dress, you could see the outline."

"Fair enough. Just remember to keep your legs crossed. I don't want you winking at me later." We both laugh. I spray glitter in my hair, grab my purse, and leave with the girls.

When I arrive at the Lion, I see Cal with his arm around Stacey's shoulder. She's much shorter than he is and the perfect height for his arm to rest there. Her bright red leather skirt clings to her chunky thighs, and the black bodice top she's wearing pushes up her large breasts, making them spill out of the wired structure.

Scott walks towards us. Stacey turns around to greet us with her smoky eyes and black lipstick. I hope she hasn't had that tattooed on, knowing she is studying permanent makeup; whatever that is. As much as she obviously likes her look, I want to just give her a bit of pink gloss. I think it would look so much nicer than black.

"Stephanie," she squeals, walking over to me with her arms open for a hug.

"Hi, Stacey, good to see you again." I pat her back as she wraps her arms around my shoulders.

She lets me go. "And you, Steph. Have you been looking after Cal for me?" She rubs Cal's arm, and I glance at him, thinking he's the one that's been looking after me.

"I was so glad when I found out you two would be at uni together. You're such a good friend, Steph, keeping him in check."

If she only knew I am a terrible person. All I've been thinking about lately is getting into her man's pants. She obviously doesn't know I caused the fight he got into last week, either. I smile at her as she takes hold of Cal's hand, interlinking their fingers, and I wish I had drank the full bottle of White Lightning now so I would have an excuse to vomit. I order a pint of cider. If I am to get through the evening with these two, I need to get sloshed.

"What's with the pint?" Cal knocks against my shoulder, looking devilishly hot as always in his black t-shirt, ripped jeans and his raven unruly hair that falls perfectly around his chiselled jaw.

"I have some catching up to do. The girls have already supped a bottle of White Lightning between them."

Cal's face screws and his lips turn downwards, sticking his tongue out as if the mention of White Lightning has conjured a bitter taste in his mouth. "That stuff's fucking lethal."

I laugh, knowing he was there that night I spewed. He was the one that took me home. "Tell me about it."

He grins and takes a sip of his pint. Stacey's hands are all over him. Her hand tucks under his t-shirt. She stands on her tiptoes to kiss his cheek and his head instantly turns to meet her black painted lips. Moving between us, she tucks a lock of his hair behind his ear. I preferred it where it was, so I could imagine it tickling my face as he kisses me. What I would give to have those lips on me right now and run my fingers along his skin.

They're just friggin' snogging each other right in front of me. "Ugh, get a room you two." I can't watch this anymore. Although I can't say I blame her, if he was mine, I wouldn't stop kissing him either.

"I've got one." Cal says coming up for air. "And I'll be using it later."

I roll my eyes and turn to talk to the girls, leaving them to eat each other's face off. I need to get laid and fast, if only to stop me having sexual fantasies about him.

Knowing everyone will move on to the next bar soon, I guzzle down my pint as quickly as I can. When we walk into the Dog and Duck, I spot Mark with his art student buddies. He waves at us and I order another pint of cider with a squirt of blackcurrant. By-passing the lovebirds, I make my way over to Mark. If I am going to get laid tonight, I figure he's my best shot. "Hi, Mark."

"Hey, Steph." He flicks his head to the side, forcing his hair out of his eyes.

"What've you been up to this week?" I take a big drink of courage. I'm going to need more alcohol before I make a move on Mark.

"Just the usual. I've spent a lot of time in the studio, which is why you haven't seen much of me this week." He leans against the bar and his shirt falls open, revealing his white t-shirt that clings to his slender frame.

"I'd love to stop by and see what you're working on."

"You should call in, I'll show you around."

"I will, next time I'm up that end of campus."

He looks over my shoulder, nodding and waving to the rest of the gang. "So that's Cal's girlfriend then?"

"Yes, didn't you meet her earlier?"

"No, I haven't been at the halls since this morning."

"Well, that's her."

"Nice lipstick." He grins, and I giggle even though I know I shouldn't, but I was thinking the same earlier.

"I think it's tattooed on." I cover my mouth before I say anything else.

Mark's steely eyes widen. "You're kidding?"

"Yes, I am kidding. I hope it's not anyway. It's friggin' awful, right?"

"Each to their own and all that." He's right. I'm not usually one to judge or call people out for their style, but the green-eyed monster in me took over. I make a mental note to stop being a bitch and be nice to the girl, even if she is slobbering all over my Cal.

A few bars later, and I move on to the cherry vodka sours. Mark and his art mates have joined our group. I walk to the bar and everything seems a little hazy. I don't even notice the bar stool in front of me and walk right into it, stubbing my good toe and cursing, hitting the stool with my purse. Cal is already at the bar with racy Stacey with her perfect big breasts and even bigger arse. At least I know he doesn't have a problem dating curvy girls. There may be hope for me yet. *Not likely, you're friend-zoned, remember*? my subconscious reminds me. That bitch won't even let me live out my fantasy without sticking her oar in. I squeeze in next to Cal at the bar.

Stacey has her arm fixed around his back. "I'm just going to the ladies." She kisses Cal again before she leaves. Ugh.

I place my hand on Cal's arm. "Are you being served?"

"Yeah, I'll get you water."

I tut. "I'm not having a friggin' water."

"You fucking are. You're wasted." His eyes narrow, and he presses his lips together.

I stomp my foot and place my hand on my hip. "You can't tell me what to drink." It's his fault I'm drunk.

"I can tell this barmaid not to serve you."

"You twat. I want another vodka sour." I slur the words.

"You're having a water, and that's that." He asks the

girl behind the bar for a bottle, then gives it to me. "Here. Sober the fuck up or I'm taking you home."

I laugh. "You will have a long way to go to take me back to Nottinghamshire."

He gives me a sarcastic smile, and I think about drinking more, so he will take me back to my room. At least it would get him away from his girlfriend.

Mark wraps his arm around my waist. "I'll take care of her."

Cal's eyes go wide as he looks at Mark, and I lean into him hoping to make Cal jealous, but know he couldn't give a shit.

"Make sure she doesn't drink any more, yeah."

"Cal, I'll make sure she's okay."

I remove Mark's hand from my waist. "Wait. I can take care of myself. I don't need either of you two to look out for me. Especially you, Cal, so you can go back to your room and fuck your girlfriend up the arse for all I care. You don't need to worry about me."

Cal grips my arm. His strong hand steadies my swaying body. I stand straight. "Because you're drunk, I will let that slide. And I will go back to my room and fuck my girlfriend, don't you worry about that."

"Well, fuck off then." I yell over the music, then turn around, and stomp out of the bar, clenching my fist around my purse. My other hand squeezes the bottle of water until it crunches in my hand. Stepping into the dark street that's illuminated by the yellow lamps, I take a moment and lean against the brick wall. My head tilts back, resting there while I breathe in the crisp air, and I close my eyes.

Through my eyelids, a shadow blocks out the light from the streetlamps. I sense him all around me. The air crackles with tension, causing the lights to buzz and I open my eyes, sucking in a breath. His hands are planted on the wall either side of my head, caging me in. He dips his head to meet my eyes and breathes into my mouth, giving me a hint of alcohol on his breath. I inhale his fresh aftershave. My chest heaves, making my breasts rise and fall in front of him, but his eyes are locked on mine.

"What's got into you?" He inches closer, our noses almost touch.

I swallow the hard lump that's lodged in my throat. "I…I'm sorry."

His eyes move to my lips, then back to meet my gaze. He breathes heavily, matching my panting rhythm. His tongue runs along his bottom lip while his eyes bore into my soul. Can he read my mind? Kiss me, kiss me, kiss me, I chant in my head, willing it as his lips move closer.

He places his finger under my chin and runs his thumb along my bottom lip, bringing a tremble under his touch. "Stephanie." My name rolls off his tongue, a whisper caressing my mouth as if licking my lips with the gentlest of touches.

The door swings open with a creek, and bangs shut again. Cal backs away. With one step, all the electricity we created is gone. Earthed and grounded, I sigh heavily. He was so close, I thought he could hear my chants, willing him to make all my dreams come true with one brush of his lips.

"Cal, here you are." Stacey walks over to us, after visiting the loo or wherever she's been—probably to apply more black lipstick—I'm sure that shit's tattooed on. She's been kissing Cal all night, and it hasn't even smudged, like its permanent marker or something. I stare at it for longer than I should, trying to figure out what it is. Where do you even buy that stuff? I know Maybelline doesn't stock it, and you wouldn't get that in my mother's Avon brochure.

Cal clears his throat. "I'm taking Steph home. She's had too much to drink."

Mark pushes through the door. "Everything all right?" He looks between the three of us.

"Steph is going home. You can walk her, can't you?" Stacey says to Mark.

Cal clenches his jaw and narrows his eyes at Mark.

"Sure. I'll walk you home." Mark places his hand on my lower back.

"Wait. I'm not ready to go yet. I want another drink. A proper drink, not a soddin' water." I wave the bottle in front of Cal and crunch the plastic in my hand.

Amy steps onto the street with Scott, both of them laughing at something, then they spot us. "What are you all doing out here?"

"Steph was just leaving," Cal says through gritted teeth.

"No, I wasn't. You were."

He flares his nostrils, wrapping his arm around Stacey's waist, which only makes the acid rise into my mouth.

"What's got into you two?" Amy laughs as we stare

each other out. "Have I missed something?" She looks between the two of us and then to Mark, who shrugs his shoulders.

I wave my hand in the air. "Cal's being a jerk."

Stacey looks at Callum and then back to me. "Callum, what have you said?"

"Don't look at me. She's the one off her fucking tits."

I turn to Mark. "Do you want to come back to my room? Amy is sleeping at Scott's tonight."

Before Mark can speak, Cal grips my arm. "I'll take you back now, come on."

Mark places his hand on my other arm. "I can take her back."

Stacey clings onto Cal's waist. "Cal, let him take her. She'll be fine."

Ugh. I walk away from the group and storm off down the street. Even though I don't want to leave, anything is better than spending another minute with the bride of Dracula.

Mark follows. "What was all that about?"

"Nothing, he just acts like he's my friggin' dad sometimes. It's annoying as hell."

"Yeah, I bet." Mark walks beside me and catches me when I trip over my feet in my heels. "You are pretty wasted though." Mark smirks, hanging on to my arm so I don't fall over again.

"Have I ruined your night? You really don't have to walk me back."

"You haven't ruined my night. It's almost midnight, Steph, the bar was shutting soon, anyway—and as much as I hate to say it—Cal's right, you shouldn't be walking home alone like this."

Everything is hazy as I walk into my room and flop onto the bed. I just need to lie here. Even though Mark is here, I'm in no fit state to make a move on him, or vice versa.

"You can stay here, Mark. Amy won't be back tonight, she won't mind you sleeping in her bed."

"I'm going if you're okay, or I can stay for a bit." I let him go, knowing I'm going to throw up at some point. The room won't stop spinning. The last thing I want is for him to see me puke. *Not exactly a great look for you.*

"Okay. I will see you Monday or whenever."

He leaves me to it. I curl up on my side, closing my eyes to stop the spinning room, but it doesn't help. My bed spins instead, twirling around like Dorothy in the twister.

CHAPTER

five

I rock up to class. Cal's sitting in his usual seat, next to mine. I haven't seen him since the other night, and I'm still mad at him. He looks up as I approach the table. I sit down in a huff next to him.

"Hey." He taps his foot, making the desk shake.

I turn my head and glare at him.

He rolls his eyes. "You're not still pissed, are you?"

"If you mean pissed as in drunk. No. If you mean pissed as in mad. Yes."

He chortles before turning into Mr Serious. "Did anything happen with you and Mark?"

"That's none of your business, but seeing as you live with him, I'm sure you already know the answer to that." Nosey twat. Who does he think he is?

He frowns. "I want to hear it from you."

"Why? What does it matter to you?"

He pulls at the metal in his eyebrow. "Because I didn't want him taking advantage of you when you were in no fit state."

I slam my notebook and pen on the desk. "He didn't touch me. Happy?"

He smiles, looking satisfied. "I'm gonna need to borrow this." He steals my pen, so I pull out another from my pencil case. Arsehole. The tutor comes in to take the class, and we don't speak until break time.

Cal stands and shrugs his coat on. "Coffee?"

"No. I'm staying here." I'm not going to the café with him, besides I want to finish my work. We only get a thirty-minute break. By the time I've reached the café, queued for a drink, it's time to come back.

"Suit yourself." He huffs and leaves with the others.

I hate arguing with him. I know I won't stay mad at him for long. It's hard to stay angry with him.

Five minutes later he returns with two take away coffees from the machine down the hall and slides a caramel bar my way. "Peace offering."

He knows me so well to get back in my good books with chocolate.

I can't stop the smile unfurling. "Thanks." We're the only ones in the class now.

He nudges my shoulder with his as he sits back down. "As much as I love it when you're mad, I hate it when you won't talk to me."

"You like me mad?"

"Yeah, you're so fucking sassy." For a minute there, I thought he said sexy. *If only.* I unwrap the chocolate bar and break a square off with my teeth. The caramel smothers my tongue in the sweet, sticky texture, giving me a mini euphoric high as it triggers all my endorphins.

"Do you want a piece?" I break off a chunk and offer it to Cal. He takes it from me and pops it in his mouth, then chomps his teeth into it and swallows. It's gone within seconds. "You're supposed to suck until it's melted and the caramel oozes out. It lasts longer."

"I don't suck. I bite." He growls and nips my shoulder, making me giggle, but the delicate bite he gave me sent tingles tumbling down to my core, and I have the urge to cross my legs to stop the throb down there.

"Am I forgiven?" His adorable grin reaches his eyes. I could forgive him anything when he looks at me this way.

"So you admit you were being a dick, then?"

"No. I was looking out for you, but I should have taken you home instead of Mark."

"I was totally fine with Mark." Although Cal's the one I wanted to be with. *He could have held your hair back while you were throwing up.* Hmm, probably best he wasn't there either. Although, he's done that many times before; no wonder he doesn't find me attractive.

Cal blows in his cardboard mug. "You could have texted me back, though. You know, that device you're so fond of with all those amazing buttons."

"I didn't even look at my phone till the next day, and I was still mad at you."

"Why did you drink so much? Even Stacey said it wasn't like you."

Ugh, every time he says her name, it's like I get a mouthful of dishwater, and I want to gag. "She hardly knows me. She doesn't know what I'm like."

"But I do. You were on a mission to get shitfaced. I

could tell when you were downing those pints. I should have told you to calm down then."

My head tilts to the side and I pout. "I got carried away. I'm sorry."

"Had someone pissed you off?"

How can I tell him? Your girlfriend pisses me off every time she touches you, and seeing you kiss her makes me want to vomit. "No, I don't know what's up with me."

I never felt this way before. I don't even understand it myself, but when I'm with him, I feel this stirring in the pit of my stomach.

He rubs his finger along his eyebrow and twists the metal ring. "Is it your time of the month or something?"

"Cal." The back of my hand swats his arm.

"What? You always get that PMS shit."

I exhale a long breath. "That must be it."

"Is that why you didn't want to come out in the first place?"

"Probably. Anyway, did you have a good weekend?" I try to change the subject. The last thing I want to talk about is my menstrual cycle.

"Yeah, it was nice to spend some time with Stacey. I took her out around York on Saturday. We did a bit of shopping on the Shambles; she loved it."

Ugh, I wish I hadn't asked. I'd sooner talk about periods again than racy pissin' Stacey. "That's nice." I force a smile, keeping my mouth closed to hide my gritted teeth.

He continues talking about what they got up to. The bile rises in my throat listening to 'Stacey this', 'Stacey that', Stacey's black lipstick was smeared all over my cock. Well, he didn't say that, but that's all I can think about when he talks about her. Everyone else enters the class, thank goodness. I couldn't listen any more about racy pissin' Stacey.

WITH A FEW HOURS of free time this afternoon, I make my way to the art studio. I need to thank Mark for walking me back to my room and apologise for being hammered. It's an old building on the far side of campus with large arched windows. As I walk by, I can see the fine art students stood behind their easels. I spot Mark in the corner and wave. He waves me in and meets me at the door.

"Stephanie, come in." He has a wide smile and holds the door open for me.

"Hi, is it okay? I don't want to get you in trouble."

"It's fine. Our tutor won't mind you being here; she's pretty relaxed. Besides, it's just free time now."

Walking into the studio, I wave my hand at a few familiar faces. Mark takes me over to the corner where he's been working.

"Can I see what you're working on?"

"Yeah, go ahead." He gestures with his hand to walk around the easel. I look at the large canvas with a sketched out drawing of York's Tudor buildings, but in a distorted surrealism kind of style. He's added paint at the top using oils.

"Mark, this is fantastic. You're so talented."

He shrugs and smiles all nonchalant, but there's a gleam in his eye that tells me he's happy I said that. "How were you the other day?"

"You mean did I have a hangover?" I pick up a paint tube on the easel and examine it. Cerulean blue.

"Yeah." Mark flicks his head, forcing his hair to the side.

"I wasn't well." I place the tube back and pick up a cadmium red.

"I should've stayed to make sure you were okay."

"No, you didn't want to see that, believe me." I snort as I let out a puff of laughter and cover my mouth. Heat floods my face. I'm sure I'm as red as this oil in my hand.

He smiles. "Do you want to do something one night?"

Is he asking me on a date? *After you just snorted as well.* "I… I would like that."

He takes the tube of oil from my hand that I was squeezing. "I'll ask the others."

My shoulders slump. I thought he meant just the two of us. *You shouldn't have snorted.* Shut up, you're not helping.

"Fab." My head bobs as I look around his workstation, trying to think of something else to say. I pick up another tube of oil. Phthalo emerald. "How do you say this one?" I hold it up in front of him.

"You pronounce it like fallow. It matches your eyes."

My lashes flutter, and I look down, shuffling my feet.

He picks up his sketchbook and pencils. "I could teach you to draw if you like."

"I doubt that." Another puff of air escapes me and turns into a snort. *What's wrong with you?* I don't know. "I'm so sorry. I don't normally do that."

Mark chuckles. "It's cute."

My insides just did a little dance, and I mentally give my subconscious the finger. He thinks I'm cute.

Mark shoves the sketchbook and pencils in his bag. "We can leave now and do something if you're free?"

"Okay, what did you have in mind?"

He smiles. "Come on."

I follow him out of the class, and we walk through campus onto the large lawn. He takes my hand and sits on the grass near the lake, pulling me down with him. The swans glide along the water, all serene, while the sun kisses my face. I lean back on my hands, feeling the soft grass beneath my palms.

He pulls out his pad and crosses his legs. "I want to sketch you."

I look around at the few students spread out on the green. "Me?"

"Yeah, is that okay?" His knee pops through the rip in his jeans, and I notice the different coloured paints splattered on the fabric.

"Er, okay." I'm suddenly self-conscious, wishing I'd made more of an effort. Running my fingers through my hair, I look down at my jeans and baggy t-shirt and suck in my stomach. "How do you want me?"

He holds the pencil between his teeth while he finds

a blank page in his book. "However you're comfortable. Like you are now is perfect."

Keeping as still as possible, only moving my eyes, my face becomes unbelievably itchy. I scrunch my nose up and wiggle it side to side to stop the tickle there.

Mark laughs at me. "You don't need to be still like a statue, just relax. You can look around and talk. I like to capture people looking natural, not posed."

I let out a puff of laughter, along with my stomach. I cant keep it sucked in any longer, it was painful. "Thank goodness. I thought I'd need to stay like that for the next hour."

He flicks his brown hair from his steely eyes, which look more blue in the light of day with a cobalt hue. "You've never done this before, have you?"

"I've never known an artist before."

"I wouldn't go that far. I'm not an artist yet." He squints an eye, holding a pencil out in front of him as if sizing me up. "Tell me about yourself, Steph." His hand is busy scribing away as he looks between me and the book.

"What do you want to know?" I relax my shoulders and tilt my head back slightly, letting the sun gleam on my face.

"I have some questions."

"Fire away."

"What is your favourite colour?"

"Lilac."

"Favourite food?"

I have to think about this one; there are so many. "Mmm, if we're talking like type as in style, I would say Chinese. If you're just talking like food item, I would say a chocolate fudge cake that's warm with ice cream."

"Nice. What's your favourite sport?"

My nose scrunches. "There isn't one."

"Best movies?"

"I like all the classics like Grease and Dirty Dancing."

"What's the deal with you and Cal?"

"Woah, you just snuck that one in there." I giggle. "Why do you ask that? We're just friends."

"I get that you're friends, but he seems really overprotective around you, like he owns you or something. I think he's a bit much sometimes. Have you dated before?"

I take in a breath and sit up straight, puffing out my chest a little. "No, we've known each other all our lives. He's just a good friend, that's all. I don't think he's overprotective. Okay, occasionally he goes over the top, but that's just his way of showing he cares." I cross my arms over my chest.

Mark shrugs. "Just an observation."

"My turn." I try to steer the conversation away from Cal, although I can't help but want to know how he feels about him. "Do you get on with him, sharing the halls, I mean?"

"He's all right. He can be moody sometimes. I've learnt when to keep my mouth shut. He called me the other night."

"When?" I pull at the grass next to my thigh.

"After I left your room, he called me, said you

weren't answering your phone and wanted to check you got home all right."

"Oh." My fists are full of torn grass. I relax my hands, letting it fall to the ground as I let out a breath.

Mark runs his fingers through his hair, pulling it back off his face. "He also threatened me."

I whip my head up. "What?"

"He said I had better not lay a finger on you, or he will fucking kill me."

"Arsehole." I pull up another chunk of grass with my clenched fists.

"He sort of apologised when I saw him on Sunday, said he was pissed and wanted to make sure I wouldn't take advantage of you."

That's so Cal. A warmth floods my body, knowing he was still worried about me even with his girlfriend here. "What did you say to him?"

Mark continues to sketch, and he shrugs one shoulder. "I told him to fuck off, that I'm not that sort of lad."

"I'm sorry, I shouldn't have drank so much."

"You see what I mean when I say controlling, though?"

I kinda like that he always does that. "It's just him and I've never found it controlling but more caring and looking out for me in a brotherly, sisterly sort of way." As I say the words, I wince. He is far from a brother in my eyes. The things I want to do to him. "Enough about Cal. Tell me, what's your favourite movie?"

He pauses for a moment, sucking on the end of his pencil. "Goonies, I like the classics too."

I smile and remember I loved that film.

Mark clears his throat. "Do you want to go to the cinema this weekend?"

I suck in a breath. Does he mean just the two of us, or is he going to mention the group again? *Play it cool.* "I'd love to go out with you. Would you like to see that new horror movie?" *I said play it cool.* My face heats again, and I put on a fake smile, waiting for his response. I know I sound desperate, but I am, let's be honest.

His eyes sparkle and reflect the lake like a French ultramarine. "You like horrors?"

"Yes, I like to watch a spooky movie, do you?"

"Yeah, we'll go on Friday, it's a date."

I bite my lip, wondering if he means date-date or a date in the calendar.

"Can I see your drawing yet?"

He turns it around and gives me a quick flash of the page. He's drawn just my face and shoulders, capturing a smile as I look towards the water.

"Mark, that's really good." I'm also glad he's stuck to my best feature and not scrutinised my body.

CHAPTER Six

Friday is finally here. With a stomach full of butterflies, I walk outside my block to meet Mark. The wind picks up, flapping my wrap dress against my legs. I pull my denim jacket closed around my chest as I walk towards him.

He stands up straight when he sees me and swipes his hair to the side of his eye. "I like your dress."

"Thanks." I smile and check out his skinny jeans and see a hint of a white t-shirt under his khaki zip up jacket.

"I thought we could get something to eat at the cinema."

"Good idea."

We start walking and Cal and Scott come in to view, strolling towards us. "Where are you going?" Cal asks, looking surprised to see me with Mark.

"Out. What's it look like?" Mark says.

Cal takes in a breath, making him seem taller. "I can see that. Out where?"

I clutch the strap on my bag. "Just to the cinema."

Cal stuffs his hands in his leather jacket. "Cool, we'll come."

"Let me get Amy," Scott says, before jogging towards my halls of residence.

Cal stands smiling at the two of us with his hands in his pockets.

"Cal," I say through gritted teeth and widen my eyes at him as if to say get lost in the nicest possible way.

"What?" He chortles.

"You're not coming with us."

"It's a free country. I can go to the cinema if I want."

"Fine, but not with us."

Mark looks between the two of us with a hint of a smirk on his face. I don't think he wants Cal there anymore than I do.

"Fine. I'll sit in the next row if it makes you feel better."

"Ugh, Cal, how can I put this politely... piss off."

He laughs harder. "All right, I get it. Don't get your knickers in a twist. I was just fucking with you."

He's such a liar. If I hadn't said anything, he would have come to the cinema and not taken the hint, or maybe he does it to be obnoxious like an annoying dad. As much as I would love nothing more than to sit next to Cal and have his arm around me, comforting me during a sad or scary film, I need to get him out of my head. Cal isn't available, but Mark is. I really like Mark, and I want to get to know him more.

Just as the lights go dim and the adverts play on the big screen, the door opens and Amy and Scott walk through with a large box of popcorn. I'm going to friggin' kill Callum after this. She waves at me and slides into the seats in front of us. My body tenses, expecting Cal any moment, but he doesn't show.

"Where's Callum?"

"He went back to the halls, said he didn't want to be the third wheel."

My chest tightens. He may as well have come, seeing as Amy and Scott are here, too. We're all friends after all. I don't want him to be back in his room alone. I text him.

> Sorry I blew you off.

No, you're not.

> Yes, I am.

You have some sucking up to do.

> Arsehole

You can start there if you like.

> Piss off.

Enjoy your date. :)

> Thanks, although it's not really a date anymore since Amy and Scott are here.

Haha

I tuck my phone back into my bag as the film starts. Settling back into my seat, Mark pulls all the classic moves. He stretches his arm and then rests it on the backrest behind me. After a while, his hand slowly makes its way to my shoulder. I lean into him. He isn't as broad as Callum and his chest isn't as taut. He's slender and his legs look skinny in his jeans. I look down at my leg and then at his, which is literally half the width of my thigh, but he doesn't seem bothered by it. His fingers graze my arm with light strokes up and down. It's nice, but I don't have the same intense tingles that I get from Callum's fingers, or the same stirring in my stomach that makes my heart race. Perhaps I need more time.

I place my hand on his thigh, and he holds it in his. The film gets darker, and I can't look. I squeeze him tight and nestle my face into his chest. His stomach and his chest quake as he silently laughs at my squeamishness.

"I thought you said you liked scary films," he whispers.

"I do, but that creature thing is going to give me nightmares."

He laughs again under his breath and my head bobs along with his chest.

After the movie has traumatised the life out of me, we walk back, leaving Amy and Scott to do their own thing.

I glance over at Mark. "I'm sorry about Cal earlier. Do you think he will be moody with you when you get back?"

He shrugs. "I can handle him."

"Really? I know he can be difficult sometimes. It's just who he is. Everything he does has good intentions, he just doesn't go about them the right way."

"Right. You don't have to stick up for him, you know."

"I'm not." I know I am, and yes, I do have to stick up for him. He would do the same for me. I won't have a bad word said about him, even though I know he can be a dick sometimes. He's my dick. *You wish he was your dick.*

Mark nods. "Right." His sarcastic tone makes my neck stiffen. Bugger, I didn't want to argue with Mark about Callum. We've had such a good night as well. Why do I always bring Cal up in conversation? *Because you lurve him.*

We walk in silence for a while. "Thanks for tonight. I've had a lovely time."

The corner of his lip curls upwards. "Even though the film scared the shit out of you?"

"Yes." I giggle.

"I'm glad."

"What, that it scared me to death?"

"I got to put my arm around you, didn't I?" He cocks his head and gives me a cheeky wink, and I look away so he doesn't see my rosy cheeks.

Biting my lip, I glance back at him. "You can put your arm around me anytime, not only when I'm scared."

He stops walking and places his hands on my waist and pulls me towards him. His mouth moves closer. He presses his lips tight against mine. Our teeth clash. I smile but try again. This time, he slides his tongue between my lips, and I sink into the kiss. It's nice, but there are no fireworks that I've read about, there's no foot popping like in the movies. My heart isn't singing and my stomach isn't stirring. Well, it is a little, but only from the hotdog I ate a few hours ago.

Mark ends the kiss with a light peck, and we continue walking the narrow cobbled streets of York. Our fingers brush against each other and then entwine as we walk to my dorm. I just need more time with him to get the feels. He is attractive. I always go for the alternative style, the grungy skater boy or the shaved head, tattooed just got out of prison look or the wild long-haired, heavy metal rock vibe that Cal has going on. Even the geeky guy with glasses does it for me. *So basically anyone*, my subconscious says. Pretty much, although I never go for the sports freaks like my brother. I hate sports.

We arrive at my block and Mark kisses me again. I hold my breath, hoping for the foot pop or the spark, but nothing. "Do you want to come up?"

"Sure."

We walk into my room, and I kick off my flat shoes. I kiss Mark again, thinking the more I kiss him the more I will catch the feels. One thing leads to another and before I know it, he's on top of me in my single bed. His artistic hands glide up my dress and rub against the fabric of my lace knickers. I pull his t-shirt up, and he whips it off. He tugs under the fabric of my knickers and puts those clever fingers to use.

It's been a while since I had some release. A one-night stand a few months ago in my hometown was the last guy to touch me here. I reach down, unzipping his jeans to reciprocate. I can feel his erection through the fabric of his boxers, and I slide my hand in to feel his skin on mine. He continues to kiss me. I wonder how far this will go. I'm not sure I want to go all the way yet. I don't have any condoms either, but I don't want him to stop. He slips another finger inside my slick folds, and I rock my hips against his hand and hope I find the release I need. A warm liquid covers my grip and Mark's frantic kisses on my face slow. He continues to push his fingers into me and withdraw, but the glint in his eye has decreased now his desire has spilled. The door handle turns. I sit up and Mark pulls his hand away.

Amy and Scott walk in. "Sorry I'm not interrupting, am I?" She looks at me and looks at Mark topless.

"No, not at all." I widen my eyes and give her a smile, but it's more of a grimace. Her timing is impeccable—first she ruins my cuddle with Cal and now she cock blocks me. Talk about a clam jam.

Amy swats Scott on the arm. "I said we should have gone to your room."

He chuckles and shrugs. "But your block's closer and I thought Steph would be out still."

He's a liar. He saw us leave. "Why would we still be out?" I can't help wonder if Cal sent him here to spy on me. But why?

Mark zips his jeans and pulls his t-shirt back on. "I'll go."

I sit up on the bed. "When will I see you again?"

"I'll call you."

I nod. *Famous last words.*

Just after Mark leaves, Scott says, "I'll head off now, may as well walk back with Mark." He kisses Amy and walks out the door, confirming he came back to spy. Scott and Cal have grown thick as thieves lately. You'd think they were the ones dating. He's probably on the phone now, texting him everything.

I throw myself back on the bed in a huff, wishing I had my own room.

SITTING in the local pub with Amy and Nicola, I polish off a Sunday roast. This is as close as it gets to my mum's cooking. I pull out my phone for the hundredth time—still hopeful for a text or call from Mark. Although, I haven't heard from Cal either. *Perhaps they've killed each other.* I smile at the thought and contemplate calling Cal just to see what Mark's been up to.

As much as I didn't get a spark when we kissed, I still want to see him again. I think it will come. I'm sure of it. As sure as Mark coming the other night. Maybe an orgasm would've helped with the sparks. Hopefully next time. *There's going to be a next time?* Well, I really do need to get laid, if only to take my mind off Cal. I couldn't even finish myself off with Amy in the room.

I wipe my mouth with the napkin. "Amy, are you seeing Scott today?"

"He's meeting me here anytime now." She washes her food down with a big gulp of WKD Blue.

My heart rate picks up a notch, hoping Cal will be with him. I go to the toilets to check my lipstick. I know we're nothing more than friends, but I can only hope that one day—and hope that one day is soon—he will see how good we could be together.

When I return, Cal is sitting at the table. His signature black style goes perfectly with his raven hair. A swarm of bees takes flight in my stomach as I walk towards him. When he looks at me and smiles, I'm buzzing. One look is all it takes. I spent an entire evening with Mark and didn't feel anything close this.

He stands so I can squeeze past him and slide into the booth. His hands grip my waist as I scoot by, making my head light. I sit down, and he sits next to me with our bodies pressed together at the side.

"How are you?" My breathy voice hitches when his hand rests on my thigh.

"Good. You?"

"Good." It comes out like a squeak. So high pitched I think the dog down the road heard me.

Amy and Scott stand and walk towards the pool table.

"How was your date?" Cal asks in a mocking tone and a snigger as he lifts his pint to his lips.

I squirm in my seat. The heat rushes to my cheeks. "It was good. Has he said anything to you?"

"No. Why?" He wipes the froth from his mouth with his sleeve.

"I haven't heard from him since Friday night. Maybe the date didn't go as well as I thought."

He slams the pint down on the table. "Did you fuck him?"

"Cal." I widen my eyes and slap his thigh discreetly under the table.

"Well?" His hand squeezes my leg.

"It's none of your business." I fold my arms over my chest. I really don't want Cal knowing what I get up to with other boys. Or do I? Maybe it would make him jealous. *Or maybe it would make him resent you.* "No, I didn't."

His hand relaxes against my leg, and he takes another drink. "He was with a girl from his art class yesterday."

"Where?"

He shrugs. "She was in his room and then they went out."

I sigh and sag back against the draylon padded booth. No wonder he didn't call me.

"He's not right for you, Steph."

"Ugh, you sound like my dad. You always say that like nobody is good enough for me."

"They're not."

"In case you haven't noticed. I don't exactly have guys lining up for me." I wave my hand around in the air.

"So you're just gonna settle and fuck whoever's available and shows a bit of interest? Even if they're a dick?"

"Especially if they're a dick. A big dick." I smile, trying to make light of the conversation. But Cal doesn't laugh and flares his nostrils.

"You need a big dick. A good fucking seeing to. It might knock some sense into you. If I was your boyfriend, I would fucking treat you right."

My pulse races and my insides are vibrating, but I'm not sure if it's excitement or anger. "But you're not my boyfriend, Cal. You're playing happy couples with Stacey, and you're not perfect either." But he is perfect for *me* in every way.

"I never said I was. I just want you to be with someone decent. Someone who deserves you, and who's worthy of you." He brings his pint to his lip and guzzles it down.

Like I don't want that too. "Well, when you find Mr Friggin' Perfect, Cal, let me know."

"I will. In the meantime, I don't want you fucking my housemate."

"I'll fuck who I want." Even though that statement couldn't be any further from the truth, if only I could sleep with who I want; it would be him.

"Go ahead then, be a fucking slag." His empty pot slams against the table.

I suck in my breath. My hand acts before my mind can think, and I slap him across the face. "You bastard."

I stand, waiting for him to move so I can get free of the booth.

"Steph, I didn't mean that. I'm sorry."

"Let me pass." The tears prick my eyes.

"No, sit down. I'm sorry." His hands are on my waist.

"Cal, let me go."

"You cannot pass.

I peel his fingers from me. "Piss off, Gandalf and let me pass."

When he doesn't budge, I climb over his legs. He wraps his arms around me, restricting me and pulls me down so I am straddling him. I scowl and push against his chest, trying to free myself from his grasp.

"Steph."

My eyes widen, feeling a growing bulge between my thighs. His fingers dig into my hips, holding me in place. I swallow. "Oh, my gosh. Are you…" Could he actually be turned on right now?

His knees pull together beneath me. "Well, your tits *are* in my face. I'm a guy. It happens." A red hue creeps up his neck, painting his cheeks, and he pushes me off his lap.

Once free of the booth, I storm out of the bar. Everyone's eyes are on me, and I need air. As soon as I burst onto the street, I fill my lungs with the fresh autumn breeze. The wind blows my curls as I walk along the cobbles. Tears cling to my lashes like raindrops suspended in a cloud.

Big arms swaddle me from behind. Cal's warm breath in my ear as his head rests in the nook of my neck. "I'm sorry, baby." That raspy voice of his makes me go weak at the knees.

I halt under his touch and let him hug me, relishing how close he is and how he makes my heart go boom. Even when I'm mad with him, I still have more feels than I did with Mark.

"I'll be buying you a chocolate bar peace offering all

week at this rate. Maybe I'll trek to the café for those baby cakes you love so much."

I turn around so I can see his gorgeous face. "All month."

He smiles and pulls me into his chest and kisses my hair. "All right, baby cakes."

The Vengaboys are back as my heart strums a new tune that goes boom, boom, boom boom. Hugging him in the street, I linger for longer than I should. The beating of his heart against my ear soothes my soul, and even though the wind whips at my hair, I'm on fire.

CHAPTER
Seven

I walk into the lecture theatre for my art history class. Mark is in his usual seat with his mates. He beams at me and nods, but his smile disappears when Cal walks in behind me. Mark swivels his head back to face the front, and I turn to Cal. "Have you and Mark fallen out?"

"No, why?"

I slide into the row several seats behind Mark. "No reason." I pull out my notebook and pen.

Cal leans into me. "I'm gonna need to borrow one of those."

"You have to be kidding me. This must be like the hundredth pen I've lent you now and I never see them again." I rummage in my bag for my fluffy pencil case.

"Calm down. I'll buy you a bunch for Christmas." He grins at me with his cheeky, adorable lips, and I dig out another pen.

"Do you want a notebook too?" I say when I realise he doesn't even have a bag.

He smiles. "Tell you what. There's no point in both

of us taking notes. Here, have your pen back. I'll just copy yours when we have to do the assignment."

I roll my eyes. The lights go dim and the lecturer walks into the theatre. "Afternoon, everyone." She walks onto the stage and places her books on the podium. "Today we're going to look at Jackson Pollock." I open my notebook. Cal leans back in his seat, making himself comfy, and places his hands behind his head.

"An influential American painter, and the leading force behind the abstract expressionist movement in the art world." She turns on the projector and a mass of paint splotches fills the screen.

Cal leans in to me and whispers, "And you said you can't paint." His words make me smile. "My sister's kid can do better than that."

"Shh," I say, but think he's probably right. We watch a video of his work and view some more slides.

"What a load of shit," Cal says.

I swat his leg. "Shhh. Art is subjective. You're a Neanderthal."

He chuckles. "Sorry, but Pollock is bollocks."

The lecturer continues. "Pollock's art has become part of the world's most expensive paintings, reaching the six-figure mark."

"Holy shit. I might take up fine art myself." He chortles. "No wonder you fancy Dick Van Dyke over there."

I knock against his shoulder. "You mean Jan van Eyck."

"Who?" His eyebrows pull together.

"Jan van Eyck, the painter."

He shrugs. "Never heard of him."

I shake my head. "Dick Van Dyke is that dude in Mary Poppins."

"Yeah, that's who I mean. Step in time and all that."

"He's an actor."

"He chalks up those pavement pictures."

I bury my head in my hands to hide my laughter, but my shoulders jiggle. I can't contain my giggles any longer.

"What's so fucking funny?"

"Keep your voice down. You're going to get us kicked out." I press my lips together to stop my laughter. I can't look at Cal. If I do, I will have another fit of giggles. And he says he's the intelligent one. Intelligent, my arse.

After the lesson, I walk out with Cal.

"Steph." I turn around to find Mark behind me. "Can I have a word?" I'm not sure I want to talk to him if what Cal said is true about him seeing another girl over the weekend. Cal scowls at him, then back at me, making me roll my eyes.

"Sure. What's up?" I say to Mark.

He looks at Cal and then back at me. "In private."

I nod and turn to Cal. "See you later." He walks off in a huff, and I walk with Mark down the path, leading out onto the green. "What do you want to talk about?"

"The other night. I'm sorry I left like that."

"It's okay." I don't really blame him for leaving after Amy burst in and killed the mood.

"No, it's not ok. I should have called you." He flicks his hair from his steely eyes.

I jut my chin out and grip the handle of my bag tight. "It's fine, I get you were busy with another girl." I won't have him make a fool of me.

He fills his lungs and stands straight, making him appear a few inches taller. "Is that what he told you?"

My eyebrows pinch. "Who?"

He shakes his head. "Cal told you I was seeing another girl, didn't he?"

"Well, aren't you?"

"She came to the halls, but we're just friends. We're working on a project together." His grey eyes have a warm hue, and I actually believe he's being sincere.

"Oh." I let out a long breath, relieved that he hasn't actually rejected me.

He shuffles from one foot to the other. "Do you want to do something again this weekend?"

My smile pushes my cheeks up. "I'd like that."

He grins and leans in to whisper, "We might get to do something alone this time." His soft lips kiss my cheek. A warm fuzziness radiates there for a split second, making me blush. "I have to go to my next class, but I'll call you Friday."

"Okay." I gently touch my cheek where his lips were as I watch him go. And he turns back to smile at me before turning the corner. Maybe I will catch the feels for him after all. I arrive at my next class and sit in my usual seat between Cal and Amy.

"I hope you told him to fuck off." Cal's dark eyes stare into mine. I don't tell him I've arranged to go out with Mark again this weekend. Cal's going to stay at his girlfriend's in Lincoln anyway, and I can't be arsed with another lecture from him. Although, I fear he can see right through me.

I pull out my notebook. "He says the girl was his classmate who he's doing a project with."

Cal huffs. "Yeah, right? You didn't believe that shit, did you?"

I shrug my shoulders and thankfully the tutor starts talking.

"WHERE'S Mark taking you on your date?" Amy scans through my wardrobe.

"I'm not sure. It's just a Saturday afternoon so I don't want to overdo it. I'm thinking jeans and a t-shirt will suffice."

Amy hands me my thin lime green jumper. "Here, this one brings out your eyes."

"Thanks." I pull it over a white t-shirt and grab my cream suede jacket.

"Have fun." She waves as I walk out the door like a proud mum.

He's waiting for me outside my halls with his backpack that he always carries. My smile widens as I approach him. "Hi."

"Ay."

"So where are we going?"

"I thought we could have a walk."

"Oh, all right."

I let him lead the way, zipping my jacket up as the wind picks up. We walk off campus past the row of trees that rustle as a gust blows through. Typical weather. It was glorious sunshine this morning. Trust it to turn blustery as I go on my date. That is just my luck. Mark takes hold of my hand, clasping his fingers in mine, and smiles. His hair falls in front of his eyes, and he runs a hand through it to move it to the side. I smile back as I gaze into his grey eyes with a hint of blue, reminding me of a stormy sea. *A murky sea, you mean.* Will you please be quiet and not spoil my date?

"So, are you going to tell me where we're walking to?"

"I thought I would take you to the wall."

"The wall?" I almost choke on the words. My shoulders tense. I'm not dressed to scale a wall. I glance down at my heeled boots. *Like you could climb a wall. Even with the proper footwear, it's just not going to happen.*

"The city walls. There is one spot where there's a magnificent view. I've been sketching the scenery, and I wanted to share it with you."

I relax my body, letting the relief fill my lungs. Wow, that's really romantic. My heart does a little swoon. I hope the wind will piss off so my hair stays nice.

"Have you eaten?"

"No, have you?"

"Not yet. I've brought food." He is definitely on a winning streak here. This date is getting better and better.

"I wondered what you had in that bag. I thought it was full of your art supplies."

He laughs. "I do have my sketchbook and pencils. I don't go anywhere without them."

"Of course. I wouldn't expect anything else." We walk to the top of the steps that lead to the stone city wall.

"I like to be prepared when I see something beautiful to sketch. And I knew today would be one of those days."

"Well, the view is beautiful up here." I take in a breath and scan the area from this vantage point.

"I wasn't talking about the scenery." He squeezes my hand and pulls me close. I suck in a breath. Our bodies collide. He holds my waist while his lips move closer until they press against mine. The wind blows wildly, pulling my hair to the side, but our lips stay locked. I feel like I'm in a movie, an adaption of Wuthering Heights, and I'm Catherine Henshaw on the moors. I get a slight stir in my tummy as I wait for a foot pop that doesn't come. Then my stomach stirs again along with a growl, and I realise I'm just hungry.

Am I flogging a dead horse here? I want the tingles and the flutters. *You want Callum*, my subconscious says. And then I wonder what he's doing. Fucking his girlfriend, no doubt with her black lipstick. Ugh. I have a great guy here right in front of me, and I'm thinking about someone who is unobtainable. What does he see in her? Is it her personality or her gothic look? If I started wearing black lipstick and smoky eyeshadow along with black leather, would he look at me differently? I couldn't do that though—I would never change myself for a boy—especially when I have someone right in front of me who seems to like me as I am.

We sit down on the edge of the stone wall, our legs dangle freely over the shallow ledge that leads to a grassy banking and open countryside in the distance. To the left is York Cathedral and the city centre and to our right is the university. He unzips his bag and pulls out a foil parcel.

"I have a ham sandwich or cheese. What do you like?"

"Any? What do you prefer?"

"I like any."

"I will have cheese then. This is lovely. I can't believe you made a picnic."

He opens the foil wrapping. "This one is the cheese."

"Thank you." I unwrap the sandwich and bite into the white bread and the red Leicester. "I love cheese."

Mark pulls out two packets of crisps. "I guess you will want the cheese and onion then?" He holds up the packet along with a salt and vinegar. I contemplate the flavours, wondering if one would make my mouth taste better than the other, knowing I am going to kiss Mark again before the night's out, but sod it. I do love a packet of cheese and onion crisps so I take the bag from him and make myself a crisp and cheese sandwich.

Mark watches me with his mouth open. "What are you doing?"

"You've never had a crisp sandwich before?"

"No, can't say I have."

"Here, have a bite, it's delish." I place my sandwich

in front of his mouth. He takes a bite, then nods his head.

"Nice," he mumbles, crunching the crisps.

"I don't think it works as well with ham and salt and vinegar though, so don't ruin your sandwich." I giggle.

"No. I won't." He smiles before taking a chunk out of his ham on white. He delves back into his bag. "I have a can of coke or lemonade."

"Wow, you've thought of everything. I like both." He hands me the Coke can. I pull the ring and bring the drink to my lips, taking a swig of the fizzy liquid.

"I'm not done yet."

My eyes widen. "You have more?"

He smiles. "The pièce de résistance," he says in a fluent French accent, pulling out a pack of Mr Kipling chocolate fudge cakes.

My chest swells. "You remembered I like fudge cake." *Oh, he's a keeper.*

"Oui."

"You speak French too? You're so smooth."

"Et ta belle."

"Wow, you really do speak French." A warmth spreads throughout my body, reaching my cheeks.

"My grandparents have a gîte in France. I spent my summers growing up over there."

"I haven't a clue what you just said, by the way. Assuming you said something's beautiful, if you mean the cake then I agree." I take a slice from the box and lick the chocolate fudge sauce that oozes from the centre.

"Have you been to France?" he asks.

"I have been to the South of France on family holidays. I'd love to go to Paris though." Crumbs tumble from my lips, and I brush them away.

Mark removes a crumb from my hair. "I want to live there."

"I can see you there working as an artist."

"That's my dream."

We sit talking, watching the sunset. Mark sketches me against the rolling hills, and it's probably the most romantic date I've ever been on. I'm really frustrated with myself that I don't have that spark, those tingles and flutters, but I'm determined to get them.

Once the sun sets, the cold air bites at my face. Mark packs his pencils away. "Do you want to come back to my room?"

A shiver runs down my spine. "Yes, all right." My voice is low and quiet, but my smile speaks for me, and Mark's eyes twinkle like the stars above us.

We walk back to his halls on the east side and into the shared kitchen.

Mark leans against the kitchen counter. "Can I get you a drink or anything? We have beers, cider, 20/20."

"I will have a 20/20, please." Hopefully, it may settle my nerves as I anticipate what's coming. Mark grabs the bottle and two glasses and leads me to his room. Walking down the hall, I can't help wonder which door is Cal's, even though he's in Lincoln this weekend. Mark opens the door to his room, and I walk in to the smell of paint. An easel stands in the corner. His desk is covered in pots, brushes and tubes of oils. An open tray of pastels sits on top of a pile of books. He clears a space on his desk, setting down the bottle and glasses and pours us both a drink.

I finger a stack of canvases propped up against his wardrobe. "Can I look through your work?"

"Sure."

I flick through the canvases and large sheets to see life drawings of large naked middle-aged women. "Did you do these here?"

He nods. "We have life drawing twice a week."

I smile, thinking how nervous I was the other week about him seeing my body. After seeing these women he's drawn so beautifully—round stomachs, large thighs, saggy breasts, so real and yet so elegant—I'm not at all worried about him seeing mine now.

"I'd like to draw you like that."

"I bet you would." I giggle to myself.

He waves a hand over my body. "You can keep your underwear on."

I glance up at him through my lashes. "Is this how you seduce all the girls?"

He laughs. "Just the pretty ones."

I press my lips together and sit on his bed, then take my drink from the desk and sip the sweet raspberry liquid.

Mark sits next to me and takes the glass from my hand, placing it back on the desk before leaning in and pressing his lips to mine. I slip my tongue in and feel the heat from his mouth.

His kiss gives me the confidence boost I need. Or is it the alcohol? "How do you want me?"

"What for?"

"To paint me. How do you want me?" My voice wavers a little, and I take another drink.

Mark's eyes sparkle "You can lie on the bed."

"Kate Winslet style?" I giggle. There's a party going on in my stomach right now, and I wish I hadn't eaten so much at the picnic, along with the fizzy pop.

He smiles. "Kate Winslet style. You have her hair." He fingers a long ringlet.

"Not the heart necklace though, unfortunately." I unbutton my jeans with my trembling hands, pull them off, and look up to see Mark sitting on his swivel chair, watching me undress. His tongue darts out, wetting his lips, and my heart races. My palms go clammy against the fabric of my top as I pull it from my head. I lay down on his bed with my arm bent and my head resting in my hand. My other arm covers my stomach, and I'm glad I put my electric blue lace bra and matching knickers on today. Mark comes over to the bed and moves my hand away from my stomach, placing it at the top of my thigh. He brings a ringlet in front of my shoulder and the lock drapes over the curve of my breast.

"Perfect." He grabs an A3 sheet of card and places it on his easel and sketches frantically. I watch in awe as his fingers work their magic, and he seems to study me, as if gazing at the Sistine Chapel. His hair flops over his eye, and he flicks it to the side. He rifles through a tin of oil pastels while holding the pencil between his teeth.

"I enjoy watching you work."

He smiles with the pencil still between his teeth, and I settle into my position.

"I enjoy sketching you." He looks into my eyes and finally, a tingle travels down my spine.

"I bet you say that to all the girls."

"You're an artist's dream, Steph."

I suck in a breath. "Why's that?"

"Your soft curves are what most artists look for in a model."

Oh, he means my fat arse, hips and big boobs. I suddenly feel a little self-conscious and cover my slightly round stomach again with my hand. He doesn't correct me, and we continue to get to know each other and talk about our families and growing up.

My mouth is incredibly dry, and I'm all out of the pink drink. "Can I see?"

"Not yet, don't move."

"I think my arm has gone dead." My hand is numb where my head rests. I blow out a puff of air.

"Just a bit longer."

"How much longer? I will get bed sores if I stay like this." I giggle.

Wiping his oily hands on an old cloth draped over the easel, he walks over to the bed, pulls a curl from my breast, tucking it over my shoulder, then leans in and kisses me. His lips are soft and sensual, matching his artistic hands. I bend my knee and feel his pressing erection on my thigh, and I get a flicker in my centre. My trembling fingers unbutton his shirt, and I run my hands over his slender body. He tugs at the elastic of my knickers and slips a finger into my slick heat, drawing the moisture from there to my bundle of nerves. I arch my back. My breath hitches. I think about touching him again, but I don't want another pre-ejaculation.

"Do you have a condom?"

He stills like a deer caught in the headlights. His Adam's apple bobs right in front of me. "I can get one."

He disappears out of his room quicker than a cartoon character, leaving a cloud of dust behind him. I lay back on his bed and make myself comfortable. I haven't slept with anyone for a few months. My heart races. I really like Mark, and I want him to like me.

He returns as quick as he left with a packet, and I watch as he whips off his jeans like a kid stripping, ready to dive into a swimming pool. My breathing becomes heavier, making my mouth dry. He pulls off his boxers and fumbles with the wrapper. After pulling the rubber sheath down over his length, I take off my blue lace pants. He hovers over me, bringing his lips to mine. His fingers enter me again, but it's more like he's stuffing a chicken. He pulls his fingers out and guides his erection into me. I wrap my legs around him and feel his body tremble against mine, and I realise he's just as nervous as I am.

He grunts into my ear each time he pushes into me. I moan, clawing at his back and close my eyes, willing my release. His movements slow down. He lies on top of me, catching his breath. He softens slightly inside of me. *Great.*

Mark pecks my neck where his head rests and then my lips before lifting off of me. He pulls out, making a squelch sound, and I'm left all flustered once again. I don't even think he realises I haven't finished. Perhaps my little moans were enough to make him think I was done. I will have to keep my mouth shut next time. *Next time, you mean there will be a next time?* I do like the guy and today has been perfect—except the last five minutes—I think his efforts earlier today have earned him another shot. It's kind of flattering that he comes so quickly, even if it is frustrating.

I smile as he pulls on his boxers. The last thing I want to do is make him feel uncomfortable. It's late now, and it looks like I will be sleeping here after all. I could crash in Cal's room. He's in Lincoln right now. No, that wouldn't be right. I'll sleep here if Mark still wants me to.

I sit up and pull on my pants and ask to use his bathroom. Mark's single room has its own en suite. In fact, this entire block is so much newer and more modern than the west block where we have to share a room and a bathroom between six of us.

When I return from the small en suite, Mark is laying on the bed in his boxers. He pats the mattress, and I lay next to him in his single bed. He pulls the duvet over us, making it nice and cosy. I turn towards him to talk, but he turns out the light, then rolls over and says, "Night, then."

"Err, Night."

CHAPTER

Eight

I wake up to a bright room. The sun shines through the gaps in the slatted blind. I look around for Mark, then hear the tap running in the bathroom. I check the time on Mark's bedside clock. It's almost 10am. The duvet drapes over half my body, and I can't believe I slept in so late. I stand up to look for my clothes. Mark walks out of the bathroom with a towel wrapped around his waist. His hair is damp and ruffled. "Hey, you're awake."

I smile. "Yes, why didn't you wake me?"

"I haven't been up long. Only long enough to take a shower." The door swings open, and a shadow forms on the floor. I follow it to black boots, ripped jeans and a black t-shirt. "Cal."

"Callum, for fuck's sake. Can't you knock?" Mark waves a hand towards the door.

Cal stands in the doorway with his mouth gaping, and something fierce glowing in his eyes as he scans my body. Even though I still have my underwear on, I feel exposed under his stare.

"Put some fucking clothes on."

I roll my eyes and sigh while I sweep the floor for my jeans.

"Here." He picks up my clothes and throws them at me.

Mark walks over to Cal. He is the same height, but much skinnier. He runs his fingers through his straight hair, pulling it from his eyes. "What do you want, Cal?"

"My fucking books back."

I'm raging inside. My blood is bubbling under the surface of my flushed skin. I stamp my foot into my jean leg.

"What's your fucking problem, mate?" Mark says.

Cal steps closer to Mark with clench fists. "I'm not your mate. Mate."

"Are you kidding me right now? Cal." I pull on my jeans.

Mark stomps over to the window and picks up a pile of books from the sill, then hands them back to Cal. "Here, now clear off."

Cal's hands turn white, gripping the books. His jaw moves from side to side, grinding his teeth. "I'll take you back to your room."

"If anyone is taking her back to her room, it will be me," Mark says.

Cal stares with flared nostrils, as if he can burn holes into Mark's flesh. I don't know what his problem is.

"I can take myself back to my room, Cal." I wrench my top down over my breasts, grab my bag, and pull out a bobble for my hair. "Mark, I'm sorry about this. I'll see you later or in class tomorrow."

"I'll call you."

Cal gives Mark an evil glare as I storm past. Once I'm out of the room, he follows me, and I hear the door slam.

"You're fucking him then?" he says, walking behind me as I strut down the hallway.

I turn and throw my hands in the air. "What is your problem?"

"I don't like seeing you get used. That's my problem."

"I told you, nothing was going on with that other girl." I carry on walking, making my way down the stairs and into the kitchen.

Cal places the books he's carrying on the worktop and then grabs my arm. "He would say that though, wouldn't he?"

"Ugh." I pull my arm away and scrape my hair into a ponytail. "I thought you were in Lincoln, anyway."

"I was. I got an early train as I have some work to catch up on."

"You don't need to act like my brother. I like him, and he likes me."

He pulls his bottom lip between his teeth and shoves his hands in his pockets.

"He's a fucking prick, Steph. You don't know him like I do. You don't live with him."

"I would like to get to know him. Cal, I'm a big girl. I can look after myself."

"I know. I just can't help looking out for you too, that's all."

"I know, and I love you for it. But you don't need to turn all Brandon Lee, Crow style on Mark."

Scott walks into the kitchen and rummages through the cupboards. "Have you seen my Coco Pops?"

Cal shrugs, and Jason walks into the kitchen. "Mark had the last of your Coco Pops yesterday."

Scott slams the cupboard shut. "Fucking liberties."

Cal smiles and a puff of laughter escapes him.

Scott opens the fridge. "I'm moving out of this dump. You can't have anything without some fucker nicking your shit. Especially that twat."

"I caught him in your room last night, Cal," Jason says as he turns on the hob and pulls a frying pan from the cupboard.

"What?" Cal shouts.

"Looking for a johnny."

Cal looks at me, grinding his teeth together again. He closes his mouth and breathes heavily through his nostrils.

"Cal, promise me you will leave him alone."

"I can't promise that."

"We should rent a house together," Scott says.

"I'd be up for that," Jason says, breaking an egg into the frying pan.

Scott pulls a pack of bacon from the fridge. "I bet Amy will move in, too. Do you fancy it, Steph? It will be cool, the four of us."

"Five of us. You're not leaving me in this dump with the rest of these shitheads," Cal says.

I tap my nails on the worktop and shrug. "I don't know. Your halls are actually decent compared to mine. At least you get your own rooms."

"Let's look for a place, then. We need four bedrooms as me and Amy will share."

"Sounds good," Cal says.

"Look, I'm going. Please don't say anything to Mark. You have already embarrassed me this morning."

"Wait. Are you the reason he wanted the rubber?" Jason asks.

"No." I eyeball Cal, pleading with him not to cause any more drama.

"Don't worry. But I'm not supplying him with fucking johnny's. He can get his own. Thieving twat."

"I'll see you tomorrow."

"Yeah, see-ya."

———

I HAVEN'T SEEN Cal today. He's skipped classes this morning. Scott said he had a heavy night. *Pisshead.* Arriving at the lecture theatre for art history, Mark is sitting with his mates. Seeing as Cal isn't here, I contemplate sitting with Mark. Sod it. I walk down to his row, and he notices me. Shifting in his seat, he half smiles and waves. I step sideways along the chairs until I reach the spare seat next to him.

"Hi."

He fidgets in his seat and sits up straight. "Hey." His friend sitting next to him nudges his elbow, then whispers something to the other guy next to him. Mark nudges him back. The entire row plays Chinese whispers. Heat floods my spine, rising to the back of my neck. My ears burn, and I wish I had sat in my usual place. I turn around and see Callum drop into his seat like a stone. He catches my eye and scowls before turning his cheek. I slink down, hoping the auditorium will swallow me up. Or maybe there's a trapdoor under this chair.

This has to be the worst decision I've ever made. Not only have I set off a chain of embarrassing whispers, I've no doubt embarrassed Mark in front of his mates, and I've upset Cal in the process. I look back at Callum, hoping he will catch my eye again so he will know I'm sorry. Right now I want nothing more than to sit next to Callum and have him comfort me, but I fear moving seats now will just cause more of a scene. Cal's eyes flick back to me and I mouth 'Hi.' He gives me the finger and looks away. I turn back to the front and sigh.

"Are you free tonight?" Mark asks, followed by a snigger from the guys next to him.

I shake my head before I can speak. "I'm working."

When the lecturer talks, I relax a little, knowing the attention will be on her, and I sink further into my seat.

"Today we will discuss Edvard Munch."

The lights go off and the projector lights up along with my eyes when I see 'The Scream' painting in front of me. Knowing Cal likes this painting, I turn around to smile at him, but he isn't there. He's gone. There's a thump in my chest like someone is hammering a wall down with a sledgehammer. The painting mirrors my raging emotions inside. I want to scream at Callum for leaving, scream at these jerks for whispering and making me feel uncomfortable, but most of all I want to scream at myself for sitting here in the first place.

"A Norwegian born expressionist painter. His work, 'The Scream' has become an iconic painting in the art world."

I stare at the painting as the tutor talks about the artist's life. My mind is elsewhere. I hear her talking, but nothing's sinking in. I can't stop thinking about Cal. If he blew me off to sit with a girl, I would be annoyed. Though he would never do that. He would drag me to sit with her too if he was that desperate to sit next to someone.

After several minutes of staring at the screen, the image has somehow morphed into a cocker spaniel with long floppy ears. The mouth is the dog's nose, and I can't unsee it now. I want to tell Cal so he can see it, too. He'd find that funny.

I whisper to Mark. "If you squint, can you see a spaniel?"

He stares and squints his eyes. "I can't see it?"

"Try again."

Mark shifts in his seat, leans forward, then shakes his head. "Nope." He half smiles, then rests his hand on my thigh.

Moving over the denim fabric of my jeans, he squeezes my leg, reassuring me of his affection and let out a breath. The light from the projector casts shadows and highlights on his face, and he winks at me, making me relax my shoulders and smile.

After the lecture, Mark stays seated, waiting for his mates to disappear. I wonder if it is so he can be alone with me, so I stay seated too.

"Are you free tomorrow?" he asks.

If only I was free. "I'm working all week but I'm free at the weekend."

"I'm working this weekend."

"You got a job?" I'm happy for him. He said he was looking for something to earn a bit of extra cash.

"I got a job at the supermarket, stacking shelves and stuff."

"What about Sunday?" I hope we can find a couple of days a week to see each other. If I have to, I'll swap some shifts around.

"I'm free Sunday evening. If you want to get together."

"I'd like that."

He glances around the room and kisses my lips, taking me by surprise. Our teeth clash again and a puff of laughter escapes me, before I ease into him and take his face in my hands. I still don't get the foot pop, but he is giving me a slight stirring in my stomach. And it's definitely not my lunch. "I have to go to my next class. I'll see you at the weekend."

"See you then."

I don't see Callum for the rest of the day. On my break at work, I decide to call him.

"What?" He answers after the third attempt.

"Where were you this afternoon?"

"What do you care?" His voice is gruff. He's still mad at me.

"Why are you being such an arse?"

"Why are you?"

"I'm not."

"Oh, come on. If I did what you did today, you

would have gone fucking mental. Shouting 'pals before gals' or some shit."

"You hadn't been around all day. If I knew you were going to be in class, I would have sat with you." There is a long pause. "Callum, I'm sorry."

"No, you're not."

"Yes, I am. Why did you leave?"

"I couldn't be arsed with it."

"It was Edvard Munch, you would have liked it." I feel bad that he missed the only artist he's ever shown an interest in.

"I couldn't give a shit if Munch was giving the fucking lecture. You pissed me off, Steph."

"I see it's my turn to buy the peace offering tomorrow."

"Save it for fucking Picasso."

"Cal, please." My voice waivers, and I choke back a sob. I hate it when we fall out.

He's silent for a moment. "Where are you?"

"I'm at work." If only I were with him right now, I know I could soften him with a smile or a hug.

"So are you two an item now then or what?"

"It's too early to say. We're just seeing how things go. I thought you were friends. It was you that brought him out that first day here and introduced us."

"Yeah, that was before I found out he was a twat."

I huff down the phone. "Why is he? What has he done to be a twat? And eating Scott's Coco Pops and stealing a condom doesn't count."

"I don't know. But don't get me started on that johnny stuff. I'm still fucking fuming about that."

"If you don't tell me stuff, I won't know, will I? I'm not a mind reader."

"I don't know why he's a dick, he just is." I can hear a smile in his voice.

"You're a dick."

"I'm a huge fucking dick."

"Cal." A smile plays on my lips as I wonder how huge a dick he actually has.

He laughs down the phone.

"I have to get back to work. I'll see you tomorrow."

"All right. See ya."

CHAPTER
Nine

I leave Callum in class while I get our coffees from the vending machine. It's easier to do that on our quick break than trek all the way down to the café. He's calmed down since yesterday and is back to his usual self with me.

Walking back to our table, I place his cup on the wooden surface. "Here's your coffee, and I got you a peace offering."

He frowns. "I told you to save it for lover boy."

I pull out his favourite packet of beef crinkle cut crisps and a Mars bar. "You won't want these then?"

"Yeah, okay. I'll have 'em." He reaches a hand up from where he's sitting, and I step back, putting them behind me.

"No, you said to give them to Mark, so I will save them for him."

He stands and tries to get them from me, reaching his long arms around my waist. "I want them."

"Too late now, you said you didn't."

He pulls me closer. His hands cover mine, gripping the items. I suck in a breath and look into his eyes. My breasts smash against him, and his warm breath rests on my cheek. He laughs, trying to free the food from my fingers. I could kiss him. He stops fighting me and gazes into my eyes. I imagine him kissing me. Those delicious lips pressed against mine, and wonder what they would feel like. The thought of his tongue circling my mouth sends a flicker to my centre, and the heat travels to my face. I gulp. Cal licks his bottom lip, then pulls it between his teeth.

"Steph."

"Hmm?" I can't form a sentence or even a word.

"You're forgiven." He leans in, kisses my cheek, and clasps the items from my hands behind my back. I release them.

"Thanks." He lets go of me after deceiving me, or was it wishful thinking? Either way, he knew my resolve was weak.

My legs turn to mush, and my limbs shake to keep me standing. How can he have such a profound effect on me? I retreat to my seat where I'd left my coffee on the table and pull out a chocolate bar of my own. My hands tremble as I tear open the wrapper.

"You all right?"

I nod and bite into the caramel chocolate bar. The runny syrup envelops my tongue and calms me.

Cal unwraps his Mars bar. "You seeing him tonight?"

"Who?"

"Pollock."

I had forgotten Mark even existed for a moment there. "You mean Mark?"

"Actually, that's a good name for him." Cal leans back in his chair, grinning.

"What, Jackson Pollock?"

"Pillock." Cal bursts out laughing, and I smack his chest with the back of my hand.

"Leave him alone. I don't know what your problem is. You're all a bunch of pussy's crying over an empty cereal box and one less condom that I'm sure you can spare. You're hardly getting any action these days—probably why you're so grumpy."

He stops laughing. "Just tell me, my rubber wasn't wasted on him?"

"What do you mean?"

He leans on the table. "Did he make it worth your while?"

I daren't tell Cal that he let me down. He would just take the piss even more. "Yes. I like him. He took me on a nice date too."

"Oh yeah, where to?"

"The city wall. He brought a picnic, and we watched the sunset."

He huffs and shakes his head. "I can't believe you put out after that cheap date."

I slap his chest again. "It was romantic."

"Sure it was. What did he pack on the picnic? A bottle of Chateau de shite?"

"No, a can of pop."

Cal bursts out laughing again. "It gets worse."

"That's enough. I'm not telling you anything again."

"I'm sorry. You're such a cheap date, Steph. You need to raise your standards."

"I like him, okay. He's nice." I sit up straight and jut my chin out.

"Nice? You describe him like you're describing your grandma's knitting."

I roll my eyes. "Whatever."

Scott and Amy walk into class arm in arm, along with everyone else following behind them. "We've found a house for rent. Are you two still up for it?" Scott says.

Cal looks at me and then at Scott. "Yeah. Where is it?"

"Just off campus. You can walk to the main street and to class, it's perfect."

"Three bedrooms and an attic," Amy adds.

Cal looks at me. "Do you want to check it out?"

I shrug. "I'm barely managing financially as it is."

"If five of us share, it shouldn't be any more than you're paying for the halls of residence," Amy says.

The tutor walks in and carries on with the corporate identity lesson. It would be amazing to share a house with my favourite people, but if things between me and Mark get serious, I wouldn't be comfortable with him coming round the house with the lads disliking him as they do. I think he's the reason they're leaving the halls. I really like sharing a room with Amy, and I don't know who else I will get if she goes. Perhaps I will get the room to myself for the rest of the year, at least.

At lunch, Scott calls up the letting agency and arranges a viewing.

"Friday 5pm is great. See you then." Scott kills the

call. His bright smile mirrors the twinkle in his eye when he looks at Amy.

She squeels and kisses his lips. "Is this really happening?"

"You need to get Jason on board. Did he say he was up for it?" Cal asks.

"He's cool. It's just Steph we need to convince," Scott says.

"I don't know."

Cal puts his hand on my thigh. "Come and have a look on Friday." Normally, I will do whatever he asks while he touches me like this.

"I'm working. Let me know what it's like." I'd love to move into a house, but I'm unsure if it's the right thing to do. It's a big commitment financially, and I don't want to have to see Cal with racy Stacey when she visits. It was bad enough going out with them. And then there's Mark.

I HAVEN'T SEEN Mark all week. He didn't call me on Sunday. Amy says he has most likely been busy with work, but I worry that he's not interested.

Cal walks into class and sits next to me in his usual seat. My eyes are instantly drawn to his mouth.

"What happened to you?" My hand automatically touches his cheek, and I run my thumb over his swollen lips and the cut on his mouth.

"I got pissed last night and fell over." His fingers

twist his eyebrow ring, then he smooths his brow with his middle finger.

"That's not like you. What were you drinking?"

"Fuck knows." He looks at Scott and then back at me, forcing a smile. The tutor walks in, stopping me from asking more questions. I bet he was stoned. Pothead.

Walking into art history class, I scan the lecture theatre for Mark, but he isn't here, which is odd. I make a mental note to call him later.

"Have you seen Mark?" I ask Cal.

He scowls. "Why? You want to blow me off again?"

"I'm just worried about him, that's all."

"He was fine this morning."

We both sit in our regular spot.

I unzip my bag. "I suppose you want a pen and notebook?"

"No, I thought we'd established I will copy your notes when we need to do the assignments." He grins, and he is so friggin' loveable. I can't help but agree with him.

Marie, the lecturer, dims the lights and starts the slide show. "Today's lecture is about Jan van Eyck."

"This is Jan van Eyck." I say to Cal.

"Who?"

"Jan van Eyck, the artist. Not Dick Van Dyke."

"Never heard of him."

"Well, shut up and listen. You might actually learn something." I knock his shoulder with mine and flash him a wry smile.

"Famous for the Arnolfini Portrait." She presses a

button in her hand and the screen shows a slide of the painting. "Signed in Latin, 'Jan van Eyck has been here, 1434.' He has also painted himself along with another figure in the mirror."

A bright light appears to the side of the lecture theatre as the door opens and closes. Mark walks in and continues past our row to his usual seat. He doesn't look around or make eye contact, and I'm slightly disappointed.

Cal whispers in my ear, "Oh look. It's Pillock."

I slap his thigh and frown at him. But he just grins with his bust lip that looks like it may burst open each time his mouth widens.

The lights come back on after the lecture. I wait, hoping to speak to Mark.

"Are you coming?" Cal asks.

"I'll catch you up."

"I'll wait with you."

I slump against the theatre wall near the door and roll my eyes at Cal. As Mark approaches, I notice a purple ring around his eye and bruising to the side of his face. "Oh my goodness, Mark. What happened?" My hand instantly goes to his cheek, and he flinches, backing up a step. I look at Cal, who is glaring at him.

"Have you been in a fight?"

He stares back at Callum, jutting out his jaw.

I look at Cal. "Did you do this?"

"No." He spits out the word.

I look back at Mark. "Did he do this?"

Mark shakes his head. "I was out at the weekend and got into a fight."

"Who with?"

He shrugs his bag over his shoulder. "I don't know his name."

"Is this why you never called me?" Please let this be the reason he never called.

"Sorry about that."

I let out a sigh of relief. "Do you want to do something this week?"

Mark's mates from the art department walk by sniggering. Cal moves his stare from Mark to the rest of the group, standing tall and filling his lungs.

"I'm working a lot this week. I'll call you."

"Okay." My voice wavers. Is he trying to blow me off?

Mark catches up with his mates, and Callum scowls at me.

I wave my hand in the air. "What's that look for?"

"You. Why do you keep throwing yourself at him?"

"I wasn't." Was I? Oh gosh, I hope I don't look desperate.

"Yeah, you fucking were. He's clearly not interested."

"Why do you say that?"

"Because any guy that's interested would call you."

"He said he will call me." Please call me.

"He said that last week, didn't he? And he never called."

"What do you have against him?"

His lips turn downwards as he shrugs his shoulders. "Come on. Let's go to class. I just don't like seeing you get used, that's all."

"Ugh, Cal. He isn't using me." Is he? He seemed so genuine on our date. *That was before you opened your legs.* I should have made him wait.

Cal drapes his arm over my shoulder. "All right, whatever you say. But don't come crying to me when the shit hits the fan."

I turn my head to look at Cal. "Why do guys lose interest after sex?"

He stops walking and places both his hands on my shoulders. "Lads who are only interested in getting their end away lose interest after they've got what they want. But there are lads out there who are interested in more than that. Lads who want to know you for you, who will appreciate how your face lights up in art history, and the way you moan when you suck on a piece of chocolate. Those are the lads you need to go for, Steph, the ones who listen when you talk, and respect you. Not trashy dicks who just want a poke and tickle."

Listening to his speech, my eyes swell. Where are these people and why can't it be Cal? Why can't he love me the way I want him to? My eyes light up for him too, not just art history, and I want to moan with every touch from his hand. Nobody makes me feel special like he does. As if I'm perfect the way I am, despite all my imperfections.

CHAPTER Ten

A week goes by and I don't hear from Mark. I think it's safe to say he's had his fun and now he's run.

Amy sits at her desk in nothing but a towel and brushes her wet hair. "Are you coming out tonight, Steph?"

I close the book I'm reading and turn onto my side on the bed so I can face Amy. "I don't know if I can be arsed tonight."

"Are you still waiting for Mark to call?"

"No." Even though I am. I had hoped he would call today. It's Friday, after all. "Shall I call him?"

She points the hairbrush at me. "Don't you dare go throwing yourself at him, Steph."

I lay on my back and huff. "You sound like Cal."

"I'm looking out for you, that's all, just like Cal does. Forget Mark, come out with us tonight."

"Oh, stuff it. Okay." I place the book on the desk and look for something to wear.

She claps her hands together and lets out a little squeak.

WE WALK INTO THE BAR; the lads are all sitting at a table. I walk towards them and Cal lifts his head, beaming as he meets my eyes. His raven hair waves around his gorgeous face and his eyes crease in the corners. He turns to Scott and says something, then he makes space for me to sit between the two of them.

Cal's arm slips around my shoulder, and I lean into him. My skin turns to gooseflesh and my eyes glaze over, inhaling the familiar scent of his body. Everyone is talking about the house they are renting. The house is already part-furnished so they don't need to buy much before moving in next week, during half term.

"Steph, it's my round. What do you want to drink?" Scott says.

"I'll have a cider please."

Cal knocks back the rest of his drink and stands.

"You sit back down, Amy will help me." Scott looks at Amy and nods his head towards the bar.

Cal hands Scott his empty pint glass. "Cheers, mate. Get us another pint?"

Amy and Scott walk towards the bar. Cal's hand rests on my leg. I don't know if it's intentional or accidental, but the pressure of his hand on my thighs somehow makes its way to my centre and tingles emerge from the spot where his skin touches mine. "Have you decided if you're gonna move in with us?"

I can't think straight while he's touching me like this. "I don't know. Ask someone else if you like."

"I don't want to ask anyone else. I mean, we don't

want to ask anyone else. We want you." He doesn't seem to realise what he's doing to me. With each stroke of his fingers against my skin, my heart does a jump to the left. I'm in a time warp. Just like the song, he really drives me insane.

"Amy said the same. I haven't worked out if I can afford it yet. I'm barely keeping afloat as it is."

"I'll pay your bond and help with your rent if you're short. I have my student loan and grant."

"You don't have enough money for me as well. Just give me a few days to think about it. I'll let you know after I've spoken with my parents."

"All right. We get the keys Wednesday."

Amy and Scott sit back down at the small rectangular table with a round of drinks. Amy talks to me, but all I can think about is where Cal's hand is and how I would love him to dig his fingers into my thick thigh and squeeze my flesh, or stroke my skin and slide his palm further up to where my legs meet. He seems oblivious to what he's doing to me and continues talking to Scott, who's sitting opposite.

The door opens, letting the autumn wind blow into the bar. Mark follows the blast, holding hands with a blonde. A chill runs down my spine, and it's not from the cool breeze. My mouth opens. I suck in a breath. So, this is why he hasn't called me. Our eyes meet, but he quickly looks away and glances at Callum, then he walks past us towards the bar, blanking me. He was blowing me off, after all.

"Steph, are you okay?" Amy asks.

Cal's hand squeezes my thigh. Something I've

wanted him to do for the last ten minutes, but for very different reasons. Now it's a reassuring squeeze to let me know he's here for me. The tears threaten my eyes. Knowing I've been used and rejected. I thought he liked me. I actually thought he liked me. How stupid.

"Steph." Cal's thumb strokes my skin where his hand rests on my leg. "Look at me, Steph." He turns my cheek to face him. My lungs quiver as I take in a breath. Cal cups my face. "Look at me."

My eyes meet his.

"Don't," he whispers. "Don't give that arsehole the satisfaction of seeing you upset."

My eyes sting and I close them to stop the tears from falling. "I just want to go."

"Come on then. We'll go to another bar."

"No, I just want to go back to my room. I'll see you tomorrow." I stand and grab my purse off the table. Cal stands, pulling his leather jacket off the back of his chair.

"What are you doing?"

"Taking you back."

"Cal, I can make my own way back. It's literally five minutes away."

"You think I'd let you go back alone?"

"Please. I don't want to ruin your night. I'm just going to go back and watch a film or something."

"Cool, sounds good." He shrugs his coat on.

I say bye to the others and walk outside with Cal. My poor judgement in men has ruined everyone's night. "You don't have to come. I'm fine honestly."

"I know you, Steph. You don't think I can see you

welling up? The first thing you'll do is lie on your bed and cry, and I'm gonna be right there with you."

I throw my arms around him, and he holds me tight. His large hands slide around my waist and my shoulders shake as I sob into his chest. His soft lips kiss my cheek.

"Come on, let's go." He wraps his arm around my waist as we walk back to my room. "He's a fucking prick, and he's not worth your time."

"Was that the same girl he had in his room?"

"Yeah."

I wipe the tears from my cheeks. "Please, Cal. Don't say I told you so."

"Baby. I'm not gonna."

Him calling me baby almost makes me feel better. "I know I'm stupid. I mean, I actually thought he liked me."

"You're not stupid, Steph."

I walk into my room and sit on the bed. "Why do guys always do this? Why am I never good enough?"

Cal sits next to me. "I don't know, baby." His arm slips around my waist and I lay my head against his chest.

"I'm always good for a quick shag, and once they've had me, they discard me. I'm never girlfriend material. What's wrong with me, Cal? Is it my weight?" I look into his eyes, hoping he will have the answers and make everything better.

"Steph, never think that. There's nothing wrong with you. You're perfect."

"No, I'm not. Nobody wants me." I bury my head in

his chest again and smell his usual fresh ocean scent on his clothes.

His fingers tangle in my hair at the back of my head and he makes a fist, tugging gently on my locks. "They do, Steph. You just haven't looked hard enough."

"Yes, I have. Believe me. I've looked." Why can't I meet someone like Cal? Better still, why can't *he* like me the way I want him to?

His thumb swipes along my jaw and he lifts my chin, forcing me to look him in the eye. "You're looking in the wrong places. If we weren't such good friends, I would have made you mine a long time ago."

My mouth opens. I suck in a breath, gazing into his eyes. Inching my lips close to his, I hope he will take the hint and kiss me. He's all I've ever wanted in a boy.

He lets go of my chin and hair, moving his head back. "But we can never go there, our friendship is too important to me."

I slump my shoulders, look down, and let out a long breath. What he's saying makes no sense to me. Surely the best relationships are those where you are best friends.

"I told you he was a dickhead, but you wouldn't listen."

"You said you wouldn't say I told you so."

He lies back on the bed with his hands behind his head. "To think he used my johnny as well."

I giggle through fresh tears. "Are you still going on about that?"

"Yeah." His biceps tense as he cracks his knuckles

behind his head, but there is a smirk playing in the corner of his lips. "What a big fucking dick."

"It really wasn't anything to write home about. It was over before it began."

Cal grins, like I've just told him some good news. "Wait till I see that little prick."

"Cal, please don't say anything to him. I'm already embarrassed enough. And don't go repeating what I told you."

I lie next to him on my single bed. He takes hold of my hand and our fingers slip through each other, gently touching as they entwine and untwine. This is better than scoffing a tub of Ben and Jerry's while watching a sad movie.

"Move in with us, Steph. It will be nice to share a house with you." His voice is gentle as his fingers slip through mine.

"All right. I will." If I can spend my nights like this, even if we're only friends, I will be happy.

"You will?" He sits up and looks at me with a smile so big his eyes sparkle.

"Yes." I widen my mouth after he has infected me with his enchanting smile.

"Sweet." He pulls his phone out and shoots a text to Scott.

She said yes.

Like he's just asked me to marry him or something. He lies back down and I snuggle into him, imagining him lifting my chin so I can look into his eyes and he says, 'Mark's loss is my gain'. His hot lips press against mine and his wet tongue slips into my mouth and swirls. My eyes open to see him still texting one of the lads with one hand.

Cal shoves his phone back in his pocket. "Do you want a drink or anything?"

"No, do you?" I could do with something for my dry throat, but I really don't want to remove myself from Cal's arms.

"No, I'm good."

"You can't be arsed to get up, can you?"

He chuckles. "No. I'm comfy."

"I'll get you whatever you want."

He holds me tighter, as if he doesn't want me to go. "I'm good." His fingers stroke my arm. "How are you feeling now?"

"I'm okay." Cal always has a way of making me feel better.

"Never let anyone make you feel like shit. There are plenty of people that will appreciate you. Never sell yourself short. You hear?"

I nod and listen to the beating in his chest. The rhythm of his heart is the sweetest sound and my favourite song.

CHAPTER

Eleven

"Jeez Sis, you've piled on the pounds."

"Nice to see you too, Seb. Still ginger I see."

Cheeky git. I've only been gone two months. I couldn't have put that much weight on. Maybe it's the pill. *Maybe it's all those late night burgers.*

"You should use the student gym."

"As if I have time to go to the gym." He's a freak of nature. Who in their right mind enjoys working out? Not the treadmill type of workout, anyway.

"Steph, you need to do something, that fast food job clearly isn't helping."

"Look, if you've just come up here to give me a lecture about my weight, you can piss off. I will move all my stuff myself."

"Okay, chill your beans. I'm only trying to help."

"Well, you can help by carrying this to your car." I hand him a large box full of books. It's heavy already and I pile a few folders on top once he has it in his arms. He seems to take it in his stride with his Iron Man biceps.

"What shall I take down, Steph?" Samantha, my

sister, asks.

I point to all the bags and boxes that line my bed. "Take your pick. All this stuff is mine."

We load Sebastian's car and I direct him to my new home. As we pull up in front of the townhouse, it looks deceiving; a small front, but there is plenty of space inside. I open the front door and walk through the small entrance hall that leads to the large kitchen with an island in the middle.

"Nice." Seb nods his head, taking in his surroundings.

Sam screws her face up. "What's nice about it? It's old-fashioned."

The décor and furnishings may be a little dated, but I imagine us having lots of parties here, with booze and pizza boxes lining the worktop. I smile at the thought and wave my hand to Seb and Sam as I walk them through the large living room. The cream carpet has a few stains along with the second hand three-piece-suite but I'm sure there will be more stains by the time we've done living here. We reach the top of the stairs, hearing movement coming from the attic bedroom that Cal's claimed.

"This is cute," Sam says, walking into my room. The guys allocated me a bedroom on the middle floor. Everyone thought the baby pink room with a rainbow painted on one wall suited me. I rather like it actually, and seeing as Amy is sharing with Scott and I'm the only single girl, I don't mind. I imagine it was a child's room previously and I don't want to change a thing, it's so pretty.

Callum stands in my doorway with a smile. Seb drops a box onto the single bed and shakes his hand.

"All right, mate."

"Yeah, I'll help you get the rest of the stuff." Cal follows Seb back down to his car to unload the boot.

Sam places a bag of clothes on the floor. "Cal looks different. I'm not sure I like his hair like that."

"Really?" That's the thing I'm most attracted to. I often fantasise about running my fingers through his hair, but I'm not going to tell her that. "I think it suits him."

We walk down to get more boxes from the car and Cal holds back for me, carrying a suitcase. "Your sister's grown up since I last saw her."

She definitely has sprouted. She was always slim and flat chested. Now she's still slim with perfectly round, large boobage. I look at Cal, wondering exactly what he is referring to; her height or her humps. "Keep your hands off my sister."

He smirks. "My hands aren't going anywhere."

"Keep your eyes off then."

He laughs. "I don't have eyes for your sister. Just an observation."

A smile forms in the corner of my mouth. If only he had eyes for me. I'm also well endowed in the boobage department, but I don't even think he's noticed.

After several trips to the car, I'm all settled in. Cal and Seb get the rest of my stuff while Sam helps me unpack everything in my new rainbow room.

"That's the last of it," Seb says.

"Thank you so much for helping me move."

"No problem. We're going now as it's getting late, and I'm going out with Justin and the lads tonight."

Sam gives me a hug. "See you soon, Steph."

"I'll be home for Christmas."

Seb bumps shoulders with me. "Remember what I said, lay off those burgers, ay?"

"Ugh, Seb. Whatever." I swat his large bicep and he chuckles.

"Laters. Come on, Sam."

I wave them off, then make my way to the attic to check out Cal's room and see if he needs any help to unpack. The door is open and I stand in the doorway admiring him tack a map of Middle Earth on his wall. It looks odd next to the AC/DC poster, but he has always loved Tolkien since I introduced him to the books when we were twelve.

"The attic room is very you."

He turns around after pressing the last corner to the wall to secure the poster. "How do you mean?"

"Dark and mysterious."

He smiles. "Your room's very you too. All sunshine and rainbows."

I love that he always says that about me. We would read the Mr Men books in junior school. He called me Little Miss Sunshine back then, as well as many other names.

The five of us order pizza and spend the evening together in the living room. Amy and Scott snuggle on the couch, Jason and Cal sit on the floor rolling up joints on the coffee table and I sit in the chair bloated after eating my greasy ham and pineapple pizza and downing several cans of cider.

"I've invited Stacey over at the weekend. She wanted to come and see the house." Cal licks the Rizla to seal his joint.

I kick my legs over the arm of the chair. "Great."

"Why are you saying it like that?" He pulls his hair back off his face as he lights up his smoke.

"Like what?" I tilt my head to look at him.

"You sounded sarcastic." He draws a long drag into his lungs.

"Did I?" Bugger.

Cal scowls at me. "If you have something to say, say it."

"I didn't mean for it to sound that way." My legs swing back and forth and a smirk forms on my face. "I'm glad she's coming over. I might ask to borrow her lipstick."

"Fuck off. I thought you liked her." Cal lets the smoke escape his mouth, making ring shapes.

"I do." My voice is a little high.

Scott leans up on the sofa, resting his elbows on his knees. "Cal, what is it with that? Does it turn you on?"

He's a brave man. I've just dug myself out of that hole, and he's jumped in head first.

Cal shrugs. "I couldn't give a shit what colour lipstick she wears. I don't mind it."

"Has she always had that look?" Amy asks.

I stay silent. I'm not getting involved in case I say something else I shouldn't. After consuming several cans of cider, I don't trust my mouth.

"Yeah, well, as long as I've known her, anyway."

Amy continues her line of questioning. "How did you meet?"

"We met at a rock club after Mum moved us to the city."

"What was it that attracted you to her?" Amy asks. I lean forward, listening to Cal's response.

"I don't fucking know. I guess I thought she was sexy." There really is hope for me. If he finds her plus-size curves sexy, he might find me attractive too, although I don't think I could pull off a black leather skirt and fishnets. It's not me.

"She is a nice girl. I didn't mean to make fun. I was just getting you back for all the times you rib me about the guys I date."

"Well, the guys you date, Steph, are tossers."

Scott laughs and quickly shuts up when I narrow my eyes at him and Amy gives him the elbow.

"Here." Jason hands me one of his make-shift roll ups.

"Thanks."

"Hopefully, it will cheer you the fuck up," Cal says.

"I am cheery," I whine in a not so cheery voice.

"Come off it. You've had a face like a smacked arse since I mentioned Stacey."

I wish Cal would give me a smacked arse. A smile plays on my lips as the thought lingers in my mind. I take a drag of the weed and relax into the chair, dangling my leg over the side, and think of all the other things I'd like Cal to do to me.

CHAPTER Twelve

The saucy book I'm reading gets exciting as the main character takes the girl from behind. I lay in bed visualising everything in my mind when the sound effects blast from Cal's attic bedroom above me. All I hear are Cal's guttural grunts and groans. I hold my breath to listen more intently.

"Yeah. Like that."

"Callum." A high-pitched voice.

"Take it."

"Oh, for fuck's sake," I say the words out loud even though nobody can hear me. I drop my book and pull the pillow over my head, but I'm slightly turned on. A squeaking sound travels through the ceiling, and there is a rhythmic knocking. I pull the duvet over my head, hoping to drown out the noise further. It doesn't work. My fingers trail down under my pyjama shorts and I imagine it's Cal's hand there sliding into my slick opening, gathering the moisture there to wet my tips and smooth over my swelling nub. I hear Cal's groans again, and it's like he's here with me. On top of me licking my ear while working his long fingers into the wet heat between my thighs. His thumb rubbing circles around me and I close my eyes, allowing myself this indulgence. It's been so long since I had a proper orgasm.

"Stacey," he groans, breaking my concentration and spoiling my moment.

"Callum. Callum. Yes." She is annoying the hell out of me and I can't finish even though I'm desperate for some sort of release and to get rid of this pent up tension. I need a man. *You need a vibrator,* my subconscious says. The banging subsides along with their moans, and I roll onto my side and try to sleep; trying to think of anything but Callum. *I need to do some laundry tomorrow. Plus go food shopping.* Maybe I will go out tomorrow night. I certainly can't stay here with these two. I yawn, thinking of where to go tomorrow evening and what the night may bring. They're quiet now and I close my eyes.

"Callum. Yes. Just there. Yes. Yes."

"You have to be friggin' kidding me." Not again. I roll over, opening my bleary eyes to check the clock. Twenty past friggin' three in the morning. Who wakes up in the middle of the night for a pissin' shag? My subconscious pipes up again. *If you had Callum in your bed, I doubt you would sleep.* True.

"Ah Stacey," he grunts, and the knocking starts again. After listening to them banging on for what seems like an hour, I throw the duvet off, jump out of bed in a huff, and stomp downstairs. I fill my glass with fizzy pop and contemplate kipping on the sofa. A large throw covers the second-hand burgundy couch, hiding the various stains from years of use. Callum's book is on the chintzy glass coffee table; a dark fantasy thriller about demons and the occult. I pick it up and settle onto the settee, pulling the soft throw over my legs. I'm intrigued to see what sort of books he reads, anything to take my mind off him and racy Stacey.

"What are you doing down here?"

I'm several pages deep into his book and peer over to see Callum walking through the living room in his tight black boxers. My eyes scan his hairy inked leg, then roam over his bulging groin, moving upwards over his tight stomach and sweaty masculine chest. His damp, raven hair falls to his shoulders, framing his gorgeous face and those dark fuck me eyes that lure me in every time.

I pull my eyes away from his glorious body and stare at the pages in his book. "I was sick of listening to you."

"What do you mean?"

I roll my eyes. As if he doesn't know. "Oh, Stacey. Yes. Yes, Stacey. Suck it, Stacey. Yes. That's it. Stacey, you're so hot. I love you Stacey and your hot wet pussy."

"Fuck off. I never said that shit." He chortles and runs his fingers through his sweaty hair.

"Not far off."

"I'm sorry. I will try to keep it down next time."

"Can you gag your girlfriend too?" I press my eyebrows together as I peer over the book at him.

He grins. "I can't help it if I make her scream."

Arrogant arse. He walks past me, heading towards

the kitchen. *Sexy arse, you mean.* My eyes follow, fixated on his buns of steel under the black fabric of his boxers.

He returns with two bottles of water. "Go back to bed. I won't make any more noise. At least not till morning." He chuckles to himself, and I throw a scatter cushion at him.

"Worn you out, has she?"

"No. I could go again, but I don't want to make her sore."

"Ew, Cal. Too much information." I wish he would make me sore. I would gladly walk around bow legged and aching from him.

He tucks a bottle of water under his arm and holds out a hand. I take it, and he pulls me from the sofa. "Come on. I'm sorry. I know how mardy you get when you're tired."

I knock him with my shoulder and frown at his cheeky grin on his freshly fucked face. He strolls in front of me, giving me a view of his muscular back. The scratches on his skin make me want to puke, knowing it's her long black nails that's done the damage. Would he be as turned on with my baby blue nails scraping down his back? Would he call my name with as much passion as hers?

"If I'm mardy tomorrow, it's totally your fault."

He wraps an arm around me as we walk towards the stairs, pressing his sticky body against mine. "I'll make you breakfast to make up for it."

I smile. He knows exactly how to win me over. I can't resist his cooked breakfasts.

———

THE SMELL of bacon cooking wafts up the stairs, stirring my senses, and I hear the sizzle in the frying pan as I make my way through to the kitchen still in my pyjamas. It's late in the morning after sleeping in, but I desperately need coffee before I attempt to get ready and function like a human. Stacey sits at the table all fuck-faced and smug with a fresh coat of black lipstick. Her straight glossy hair is black as night, making her look like Morticia.

"Morning, Steph," she sings and takes a sip of her orange juice. Why is she so cheery? *Probably because she was well and truly ploughed several times last night.* Yep, that'll do it. Cal is turning the bacon in the pan, wearing a pair of joggers and nothing else. His wet hair drips onto his magnificent torso, making the skull tattoo at the top of his arm look like it's weeping.

I rub my eyes and yawn. "Morning."

Cal turns to me and puts an arm around my shoulder. "Are you still grumpy?"

Stacey giggles, covering her black mouth with her anthracite fingernails.

"Yes." I narrow my eyes at him, but I can't hide the smile that forms when he kisses my messy hair at the side of my head.

"Sit down. I'll make you some coffee," Cal says, using the spatula to gesture towards the table.

"Thanks, but you shouldn't be cooking bacon shirtless." I pull Amy's apron from the draw. It's pink with a cup cake design that says whip it good on the front. "Here." I pop it over his head and he smirks. "Turn around." I tie it at the back, getting a good look at the scratches there and know a few bacon splatters won't bother him. "All done." I pat his back before sliding into the seat opposite Stacey.

"What do you want for breakfast?" Cal asks.

I wave a hand in the air. "Whatever you're cooking."

"I'm having bacon and egg, but Stacey's having poached egg on toast. I can do you your favourite scrambled egg with cheese."

"No, Cal. Don't go to any trouble. I will just have a bacon and egg sandwich, same as you. You're already doing two different meals."

"I don't mind taking care of my girls." Stacey shifts uncomfortably in her seat and the smile disappears from her face. Did she not like him calling me his girl? She can piss off. I was his girl before she came along, and I will always be his girl, even if I am just a friend.

"How long are you staying, Stacey?"

"I'm going back to Lincoln tomorrow." Great, I have another night of listening to them acting out the Kama Sutra.

"Are you going out with Amy tonight?" she asks.

"I don't know. Are you?"

"No, well, we were hoping for a night alone." She twists the glass of orange juice around with her fingers and glances at Cal, flashing him a shy smile. Bitch. Of course, you want to get him alone so he can shag your brains out again. I force a smile and look at Cal as he breaks an egg into the pan. There's no way I'm staying in tonight with the lovebirds.

"Okay, I'll go out."

She smiles and glances at Cal again. He gives her a wink. Just let me vomit now.

"Make sure you get all your shagging done before I get back."

Cal laughs and hands me my sandwich.

"Thank you."

Stacey looks smug. I wonder what she has planned. What was he doing to her last night to make her scream his name? I don't recall anyone ever making me come so fiercely.

I CAN'T WAIT to escape the sickeningly sweet atmosphere around Cal and Stacey. Amy, Scott, Jason and I leave the house early in the evening and head straight to the first bar on the way to the main drag.

Jason goes to the bar to get the first round of drinks, while the rest of us sit at our usual table. "Amy, could you hear them last night?"

"No, I must have slept through."

"Who are you on about?" Scott asks.

"Who do you think? The happy couple, of course." The words leave a bitter taste on my tongue.

Scott smirks. "Could you hear them going at it?"

"Er, you could say that. All friggin' night."

Scott chuckles. "That's my boy."

I roll my eyes.

Jason comes over with a tray of drinks.

"Could you hear Cal and Stacey going at it last night, Jason?"

"I didn't hear a thing, but the attic is above Steph's bedroom, isn't it?"

Scott takes his pint from the tray. "To be fair though Jase, a bomb could go off and it wouldn't wake you up."

Amy looks at me. "Don't you like her?"

"I don't mind her. Why do you ask that?"

She shrugs her shoulders and sucks on the straw that's in her bottle of WKD Blue. "I just got that vibe."

"I was just pissed off listening to them all night, that's all."

"You need a good shag." Jason leans close to me, raising his eyebrows and wiggling his tongue.

I push him away. "Gross."

"Why not? We can be friends with benefits." He wiggles his eyebrows again.

"I don't think that's a good idea."

Scott laughs. "Look how that worked out last time."

I squish my eyebrows together. "What do you mean?"

"Oh, nothing. Just that painter dude."

"Oh yeah, Cal was pissed. I don't want to get on the wrong side of him."

I take my cider from the tray in a huff. "Why is everyone so friggin' scared of Callum?"

Scott puts his drink on the table and leans forward. "Have you seen him in action?"

"She wants to see him in another type of action," Amy says with a hint of a grin.

I smile at her, knowing she's right, and quietly sip my cider.

"She isn't denying it," Scott shouts.

"Well, if you'd heard them last night, you would be the same. I want to know what he was doing that made her scream."

Jason puts his arm around me. "Do you fancy him? You can tell us."

I glance at him and then at Scott, who leans over, waiting for my answer. "Come on, tell us. Do you?"

I can't tell them. I don't trust them to keep their mouths shut. "We're friends, that's all."

"But would you like it to be more than friends?" Scott looks at Jason as if they know something I don't. Gosh, they must know I fancy him. Is it that obvious?

"If Callum asked you out, would you say yes?" Jason asks. Scott licks his lips, leaning on the edge of his seat.

I put on my best poker face, but my cheeks are on fire. "No, we've been friends like forever. Plus, he has a girlfriend."

"Fair enough." Jason lets go of me and reaches for his pint.

I can't be honest with them. If Callum found out I fancied him, I would die of embarrassment. It would certainly make things awkward between us, especially as we are now living together.

CHAPTER

Thirteen

S tepping out of the bar, I wish I'd brought a jacket; the wind has picked up and bites at my skin. I wrap my arms around my body as we walk to the next bar.

Scott holds the door for us to step into a lively atmosphere with a tropical theme.

We all make our way to the bar. A neon cocktail sign flashes in my eyes. But I want the strong stuff. "Who's having shots?"

Jason flinches his head back. "Bit early for shots, isn't it?"

"It's never too early for shots. I need to get wasted tonight. I don't want to be hearing our resident nymphomaniacs giving out tips on the art of pleasure."

"I'll help you find someone, Steph," Amy says. "You deserve a bit of fun of your own after all that Mark business."

"Thanks, Amy. I'm still having that shot though."

"Me too." She giggles.

Several shots, ciders and pubs later, we walk into

my favourite 80s bar. Amy and I go straight to the dancefloor, leaving the lads to get a round in.

'Love is a Battlefield' plays by Pat Benatar. "I love this song," I shout over the music to Amy. Closing my eyes, I sway to the music. Familiar hands slide around my waist from behind and my breath hitches. Callum? A smile forms as I turn around, but it disappears as quickly as it came when I see another guy with dark hair and dark eyes. Much shorter hair than Cal but wavy on top and he looks older, mid-twenty's for a guess.

"Hey, I'm James. What's your name?" he says into my ear, still holding on to my waist.

"Stephanie."

"Can I get you a drink?"

Jason interrupts and hands me a cocktail. James removes his hands from my waist. Jason looks back at me with an eyebrow raised.

"Thanks, Jason."

"Sorry, pal," James says and walks away.

I huff and slump my shoulders.

Jason stands looking puzzled. "What was that about?"

"He thinks you're my boyfriend. I was just about to pull as well."

"Oh, shit. Sorry. We can still be friends with benefits." He wiggles his eyebrows.

I swat his arm, but know he's only teasing.

"Last chance before I pull that blonde bird at the bar." He points to a bunch of girls.

I giggle. "Not a chance."

"Your loss. I'll use my charms on someone else." He winks before turning away to try his luck. I know he's only teasing me, there's no chemistry there whatsoever. I look around for James.

Amy is with Scott, sucking on a Pina Colada. "Steph, that guy is at the bar." She practically shoos me off the dancefloor in his direction.

I shuffle through the crowd to stand next to him. "Hi."

"Hey."

I bite my lip and tap my fingernails on the bar where he stands. "I don't need a drink but you can walk me home if you like." The alcohol has made me brave, along with my desperate need to have some relief and feel loved again.

He flinches his head back and furrows his eyebrows. "What about your boyfriend?"

"He's just my housemate."

He smiles and leans against the bar. "You're a student?"

I sip my fruity cocktail. "Yes. What about you? What do you do?"

"I'm an IT consultant. I fix computers."

"Oh, that's handy. I actually have a problem with mine."

He steps closer and moves his hand to my waist. "I can take a look for you."

I twirl the little umbrella in my drink. "Great, when you've seen to me, you can see to my computer." I smile and look into my cocktail and bite down on the straw. I glance back at him to see his eyes wide and a smile has taken over his face, like I've given him tickets to a computer convention. He's dressed smart and looks kind of geeky but sexy at the same time like Bruce Banner before he Hulks out.

"I like a girl that knows what she wants and isn't afraid to say it." He takes a long drink from his bottle, then places it on the bar. "Are you ready to go?"

I check the time on my watch. It's almost midnight. Hopefully, I've missed the reenactment of Boogie Nights back at the house. "Let me just tell my friends I'm leaving."

He nods and I suck up the last of my cocktail, while I find Amy and Scott on the dancefloor. Jason is too busy copping off with a blonde to notice me.

"Amy, I'm going back."

"Do you want us to come home with you?"

"No, James is walking me home." I smile and tilt my head slightly, flashing my eyes towards the bar at James.

Amy's eyes sparkle as bright as the fluorescent disco lights. "Have fun."

"I will. See you later."

I take hold of James' hand and we walk out of the bar into the cool night air.

"Where are you staying?"

"Not far, it's—" I can't get my words out in one sentence with my intermittent hiccups. "Towards campus."

"What are you studying?"

Another hiccup. "Marketing." My foot trips over my

other, making me stumble in my heels. James catches me and I giggle.

"Are you okay?" His smiling face comes into focus. "I looked at marketing."

"Did you study here?" I hiccup out the words. Why did I drink so much?

"I went to Oxford."

"Oh, really. You're a posh boy?" I bump shoulders with him and stumble again.

"Hardly. I'm a Yorkshire lad. I grew up around here. Do I sound posh to you?" He has a cute grin that makes my stomach stir.

I glance down and then back at him. "A little, but I love a Yorkshire accent."

"Where are you from originally?"

"Nottinghamshire."

"My own Maid Marion." His hand squeezes my fingers.

I gaze at him with a smile playing on my lips. He stops walking and pulls me into a shop doorway, pressing his body against mine, catching me off guard. His lips smash into mine and his tongue vigorously laps my mouth, in total control and has me at his will. A tingling blossoms in my centre. I want to rip his clothes off and see what's underneath his pristine blue shirt. *Then why are you wasting time in this doorway?* Because his lips feel nice, and I can't seem to move my legs, but I do have an ache in me that needs taking care of. James must read my mind as he takes my hand again and we continue to walk down the street. My mouth hasn't closed since he ravished me, and I no longer have the hiccups.

He smiles and squeezes my hand. "We can go back to my place if you like. I share a house with a colleague but he's out tonight."

I think about it for a moment. I hardly know him, he could take advantage of me. *You're gonna sleep with him, anyway*. He could be a murderer or whatever. No. I would feel more comfortable at home with the others there.

"It's okay. I'm just around this corner. I have my own room."

We arrive at the house. I unzip my bag and rummage for my key. "It's in here somewhere." I pull out my coin purse and hand it to James, then tuck my huge phone under my arm. I place my lipstick between my teeth. The compact mirror slips down my bra. I hold the eyeliner in my hand.

"How much stuff have you got in there, Mary Poppins?" Not another one that likes to reference that film. I smile, remembering Cal going on about Dick Van Dyke. My fingers feel inside my almost empty bag, gliding against the silky lining.

"Found it." I take the key and line it up with the lock and miss. It's like there are three of those things. I must be drunker than I thought. The yale lock swirls around on the door and I chase it with the silver key in my hand. It just won't stay still. I giggle and James joins in with my laughter. I jab the key into the hole and it darts to the side, scratching the wooden door. After my fourth attempt, James takes the key from me, handing me back my purse. He unlocks the door on the first attempt. My eyes widen I'm in awe of his skills.

"You're good at putting things in holes." I slur the words a little and giggle again. He bursts out laughing, and I put my finger to my lips, shushing him to be quiet. Though I think my loud shushing noises are louder than his laughter. "You have to be quiet. We don't want to wake Dirk Diggler and his co-star."

"Who the hell is Dirk Diggler?"

"Never mind." I burst out into a fit of laughter again. James is now telling me to be quiet, putting his finger over my lips before silencing me with his mouth.

The house is eerily quiet, or am I too drunk to hear anything? "This way." I whisper loudly, leading James up the stairs. Tripping on the top step, I fall onto the landing at the top of the stairs. As I turn around, James is walking up. I pull him onto me and kiss his lips. The flicker returns in my core, and I can't wait to tear his shirt off. He stands and pulls me up with him. I hold my breath as we tiptoe towards my room, listening out for Morticia and Gomez, but hear nothing, thank goodness.

I open my door and tug on James' shirt, pulling him through the threshold into my bedroom. Softly closing the door behind me, my lips collide with his once more, and he pushes me backwards until I fall onto my bed. He climbs on top of me. I reach for his belt, but my fingers don't work, and I fumble with the buckle. He laughs into my mouth before rolling off me to lie on his back and undoes it for me. I sit up and watch in anticipation as he unbuttons his jeans, and then the zipper. My mouth waters, waiting to see what's lurking behind his denim prison. He lifts his arse off the bed and pulls his boxers and jeans down in one full swoop. His erection nods at me, winking almost. James leans up on his elbows, and I hover over him, kissing his lips. Moving down to kiss his slender body, I work my way to his erection and take him in my mouth. I lick the tip while sucking, and hollowing my cheeks.

"Ah, Stephanie. You're good. So good."

Still fully clothed, I slide my wet panties from my legs. My core is practically screaming his name and drooling over him. I climb on top, desperate to get my fill, and play with my new toy. I hover over him and try to align his erection into me.

"We're not going to have another key and lock situation, are we?" He chortles. "I know your skills are limited when it comes to positioning things into small holes."

I giggle. "I think I can manage this." My sex grinds against him. The tip of him pushes through my tight muscles that are throbbing from him.

"Wait. I need a condom," he says.

Oh no. Not this again. "Please tell me you have one." There is no friggin' way I am borrowing one from Callum. I still haven't heard the end of that.

"Yes. In my wallet in my jeans."

Thank goodness. I climb off and pick up his jeans and hand them to him. He quickly pulls out his wallet and retrieves a shiny wrapper.

"Do you want me to put it on for you?"

"Best let me. I'm not sure you're capable after the

key situation." He laughs again. Ripping open the packet and rolls the pink cover over his length, then beckons me back on top of him. I climb on like a kid in a playground full of excitement at sliding down the pole. He helps align himself to me and I moan as the tip pushes past my entrance. I rock my hips as if I'm riding a rocking horse. He hits all the right spots. His hands clench my thighs, and he groans, making me lose all control as his deep guttural voice rocks through me. I call out his name, not worried about being quiet. In fact, I make it my mission to be as loud as possible.

"James. James."

"That feels so good."

My hips rock faster. "James, you feel so good."

I pant, the pleasure tingles through me. My sensitive spot rubs against his groin while he fills every part of me.

"Stephanie, you're fucking amazing."

"James, tell me more."

"I knew you would be good in bed when I saw you shaking your arse on the dancefloor." His large hands grab my arse cheeks, and I moan again.

"And these knockers. You have amazing big tits." His hand rides up my top and palms my breast.

"I'm coming." I hold on to the fabric of his shirt and realise I was so desperate, I never even got to take it off. My legs turn to mush. I stop rocking as if my mind has left my body, and I'm soaring high on a park swing.

The swinging slows, and I look down at James, licking his lips. "I haven't finished yet." He rolls me over, pulling out of me and then flips me on my front.

Lifting my skirt back up to get a good view of my arse. I didn't expect him to be so forceful. He rams into me from behind, pushing me forward. My head hits the headboard.

"Oh gosh. James." I cry out with every thrust, which only spurs him on.

He grunts again, then eases out of me. I turn around to sit on the bed, hoping for a kiss and a cuddle. He takes the condom off, and I point to my small bin in the corner of the room. I lay blissfully dazed, still catching my breath.

James pulls his boxers on.

"Are you not staying?" I sit up and fluff the pillow.

"No, I like my own bed."

I slump against the headboard. "Will I see you again?"

"I'm out most weekends."

"Right." That means no, then.

"I'd like to get together again for sure."

My smile pushes my flushed cheeks up. So he does want to see me again. "Me too. I've had a really good time."

He steps into his jeans. "So have I. You're a real go-er. I love how confident you are. Most fat girls are shy."

My mouth opens. Did he really just say that?

"You're really pretty too, despite your size."

Despite my size? The words ring in my ears. My chest tightens and I want to scream. "I can throw a good punch too, thanks to my size."

"Woah, sorry, I didn't mean it like that. I'm just giving you a compliment."

I fake smile with gritted teeth. Not really knowing what to say or how to come back from that. My hand strokes my throat. I think it's safe to say I won't be seeing him again. *Unless you're desperate.* I will never be that desperate to sleep with him again.

Once he's zipped up his jeans, he nods to my desk. "Do you want me to take a look at your computer?" Like what he's just said is totally acceptable. Is he for real?

I stand and open the door to my room. "It's fine. I'll see you out. I'm sort of tired now, being a fat girl and all."

"I didn't mean to say fat. What I was trying to say was that bigger girls are always more fun in the sack."

"Oh my gosh, just stop talking and clear off. If I never see you again, it would be too soon."

He puts his wallet back in his pocket, and I can't get him out of the house fast enough. I fix my clothes and walk him to the front door. We don't speak. I can't be arsed to get into an argument. He's not even worth it. I lock the door after he's gone. I want to cry. *At least you got an 'O' out of it.* I needed that, but it doesn't seem worth it now to be left feeling fat and worthless. I run the tap for a drink, but just stare, mesmerised by the constant flow of water that's never ending; like my life really; a constant flow of jerks that always disappoint me. Will it ever end? Why doesn't anyone ever want me? All I want is to feel loved and be accepted as I am by somebody who wants to have a proper relationship with me.

I'm so lost in my own thoughts I don't hear Callum

walk into the kitchen. He pulls a glass out of the cupboard and holds it under the running tap, scowling at me. I really can't be doing with him now; or anyone, for that matter. I just want to crawl back to my room, curl up into the fetal position and hope I can be reborn as someone else.

"Has boy wonder gone?"

"No." I'm not sure why I lie, but my mouth spoke before his question registered.

He takes a big gulp of water and glares at me over the pint glass.

Why is he being such a miserable bastard? "What's up with you? Racy Stacey not putting out tonight?" I fill my glass up and turn the tap off.

"Oh, she's put out all right. I've worn her out. She's sleeping." I scan his chest and get a good look at the purple mark she's no doubt gave him with her thick jet painted lips. "So why are you so friggin' miserable?"

His jaw clenches. "Because I was woken up to you screaming the fucking place down. Was that for my benefit? Were you trying to get me back for last night? Because that's just fucking childish."

"I don't know what you're talking about." I take a drink of my water.

"Oh… Yes… You feel so good. Harder."

I'm glad he heard.

"What was he doing that was so fucking good you had to make so much fucking noise?"

"I could ask you the same question."

"Who was it? Not Mark? If he's up there I'll fucking kill him."

"Of course it's not Mark." Jeez. I know I was desperate, but I do have some dignity.

"Who then?" He grips my arm tight. His eyes dark and dangerous.

"No one you know. Anyway, I best get back for round two."

He lets go of my arm. "Keep it fucking down."

I grab another glass of water as though I'm taking my non-existent lover a drink.

"I can't promise anything." I walk out of the kitchen with my hands full and don't look back. My shoulders shake when I get to my door, and I place the water on the desk. Dropping onto my duvet, I silently cry into my pillow. I want to be a strong independent woman who doesn't need a man to make me feel good about myself. The highs aren't worth the lows that follow, each one drops me deeper into despair and I worry I'm losing myself.

CHAPTER
fourteen

I sit in class with Cal on our coffee break. "Are you doing anything this weekend?"

"I might go to Lincoln to see Stacey." He stirs the coffee in the paper cup.

I lean back in my chair and twiddle my pen between my fingers.

"What about you? Are you seeing James fucking Bond this weekend?"

I take in a deep breath and exhale. "No."

"Why not? Did he leave you shaken, not stirred?" He titters.

"Something like that." I shrug and look down at my desk.

He mocks my voice. "James, you're so big, you make me come so hard."

"Piss off." I swat his chest.

"Lame James has a good ring to it, don't you think?" He picks up his coffee, blowing into the cup.

I use my hand to wave between us. "Why do you always make fun of the people I date?"

He shrugs. "Because I like to wind you up." He sips

his coffee, and I hope it burns his tongue to stop him from mocking me further.

"Well, I won't be seeing him again." I spin the pen on the table.

"Why not, if he was so fucking fantastic?"

I stop the pen from spinning and turn to face Cal. "He basically said I was fat-tastic." My voice is quiet.

He places the coffee cup down and grips the edge of the table. "You're fucking kidding me?"

"Big girls are go-ers, apparently." I look down and pick at the hem of my top.

Cal's rough fingers lift my chin. "He said that?"

"Something to that effect."

"Who is he? I want you to point him out on campus." His jaw moves from side to side, and I can hear his teeth grinding together.

"He isn't on campus. He's older, he works in the city." My hand waves in the air in the direction of the city centre.

Cal's eyes fix on mine and his nostrils flare. "Where?"

"I don't know."

"I'll rip his fucking head off for saying that about you." Cal's fist clenches, and I hear his knuckles crack.

I place my hand over his fist, trying to calm him. "It's fine. You don't need to fight my battles all the time. It's over. He was good in bed, but his social skills left a lot to be desired."

"Steph, why do you always sleep with people who don't appreciate you?"

"Oh, he appreciated me. He appreciated my fat arse. He just didn't want to take it out in public with him."

Cal's arm goes around my shoulder as he pulls me into him and kisses my head. His fingers graze my arm, and it's like a flutter of butterflies kissing my skin.

Everyone arrives back in class, and we resume our business studies lesson.

That afternoon, we go to our art history lecture. I ignore Mark and his friends, and he ignores me, too. Cal glares at him as if burning lasers into the back of his head. It makes me smile how he has such resentment, when it was me he hurt. All he did to him was steal a condom. The tutor walks in and turns on the projector. My eyes light up when Michelangelo appears on the screen.

"Today we are going to talk about arts' most famous treasures." She presses a button to reveal the next slide. "Michelangelo's Creation of Adam. A fresco painting that forms part of the Sistine Chapel ceiling."

I lean forward in my seat, soaking up the picture and all its details.

Cal leans forward and whispers, "What's going on with Adam's pecker?"

I turn to him and roll my eyes. "You're so immature."

He silently chuckles, jiggling his shoulders next to mine.

The tutor continues, "The painting captures the scene of God breathing life into Adam who was to become the first man and was later joined together with

Eve who helped to start off the human race as we know it."

"He needs to breathe some life into that member of his."

I knock Callum's shoulder. "Shh."

He smiles, resting his hands on the seat in front. I place my hand next to his, almost touching his fingers. The electricity between our two hands resembles the painting on the screen. My little finger brushes against his and with each caress of his skin, Callum breathes life into me. He livens up every cell in my body until he has its full attention. Even my nipples stand erect at the touch of his hand. I stare at him instead of the screen. He's exquisite. A masterpiece in his own right. He's Van Gogh's Starry Night; a dreamy, heavenly image. A bright light and beacon of hope; someone I know will always be there for me as sure as the stars in the sky.

We may not be boyfriend and girlfriend, but he's always there for me when it counts and maybe that's why I love him so much. He's the only person to make me feel loved unconditionally. Other than my family and even they've had their moments, always going on about my weight. But with Cal it doesn't matter how many burgers I eat, or whether I've washed my hair. He always has a smile for me and a way of making me feel beautiful.

"Is Cal here today?" The tutor asks.

"He's not feeling well, sir." Really, he's skipping

class to go to Lincoln to visit Stacey. He only saw her last weekend. Talk about loved-up. It makes me want to retch.

After class I go to work but finish early with stomach cramps. I get the bus home and crawl into bed with my paracetamol and a hot water bottle on my stomach, hoping it will take the period pains away. I hate my life.

My phone rings. I roll over and look at the screen to see Stacey's name flash up. I only have her number because Cal used my phone once to text her when he ran out of credit. Thinking Cal is using her phone, I swipe to answer. "What's up?"

"Steph. It's Stacey."

I sit up, throwing the duvet off me. Why is she calling me?

"Is Callum there?" Her voice wobbles.

My heart races. "No, he was coming to visit you." A lump lodges in my throat. "Has something happened?"

"Damn right something's happened."

My chest collapses inwards. *Please let him be okay.* "What? Tell me."

"You must know. He tells you everything. You're his best friend." Her voice is condescending.

"I don't know what you're talking about. Just tell me, is he okay?"

"He broke up with me."

"What?" I suck in a breath.

"He left about an hour ago. I thought he would be back now. He won't answer my calls."

I let out a sigh of relief and take several deep

breaths. "You had me worried. I thought something had happened to him."

"Something has happened to him. He's lost his damn mind. Is he seeing someone else?"

"Not that I know of." *I hope not.*

"Why would he end our relationship?"

"I don't know, Stacey. He hasn't said a word to me about it."

"I don't understand. We had such a good time last weekend, probably the best sex of my life."

Oh gosh. TMI.

"And now he ends it without even an explanation." I can hear a slight break in her voice and I'm a little sad for her.

"What did he say?"

"He said he doesn't want to be with me anymore, that long-distance relationships aren't his thing."

"I'm sorry." *No, you're not.*

"Will you talk to him?"

"Sure." Although I'm not sure what she wants me to say. I won't convince him to go back with her. Maybe now is my chance. *You're friend-zoned, though.* Shut up.

"Thanks."

"Bye, Stacey." Why didn't he say anything to me? I lie back on my bed, my cramps forgotten.

"Steph." Cal's voice sounds, and my door opens. I roll over and see him standing in my room. "Amy said you weren't feeling well."

"I'm okay now."

He walks in and sits on the bed next to my legs and

places his hand on top of the hot water bottle that rests on my stomach. "Can I get you anything?"

"I wouldn't mind a cup of tea."

He shifts on the bed and pushes himself up. I hold his hand. "Wait. Don't go yet. Stacey called."

He leans back on the bed and lets out a long breath. "What did she say?"

"That you broke up with her." I pull myself up and lean against the headboard.

Cal nods. "Did she sound okay?"

"Not really. She was pissed. What happened? Did you have a row or something?"

He shakes his head. "I went there on purpose to end it. I couldn't string her along any more. It wasn't working for me."

"But after last weekend? I thought everything was great between the two of you." I look at him, confused. He isn't really giving much away.

"I just can't be arsed with a long distance relationship."

"I hope it's not because of what I said the other week. I don't dislike her."

A puff of air escapes his lips. "It's nothing to do with you, Steph. I'll make you a cuppa."

CHAPTER

Fifteen

C al comes back with a cup of tea, just how I like it. "Dean's coming over. He's on the road now."

I sit up and take the hot cup from him. "Dean from school?"

"Yeah, he bought a car today."

"Oh, that's great. Is he staying for the weekend?"

"Yeah, we'll probably go out tomorrow, but tonight I think we'll just order a pizza and have a few beers."

There's a knock at the door. "That'll be him now. Come down when you're ready and hang with us."

"Okay."

After drinking my tea, I walk downstairs and outside to Cal and Dean, checking out his car parked in front of the house. The street lamp illuminates the black Fiesta. "Hi, Dean. When did you pass your driving test?"

"In the summer. I've been saving up to buy a car. Borrowing my mum's Fiat was cramping my style. Wanna go for a ride?" He raises his eyebrows and nods towards his car.

Cal's sitting in the driver's seat. He leans over the

centre console and shouts, "I'll take her for a ride. Get in."

I still have my slippers on, but what the heck. Dean opens the door, and I jump in the back seat. "I didn't know you could drive, Cal."

Dean gets in the passenger side. "He can't drive."

Cal shrugs his shoulders. "How hard can it be?"

Oh no. "You have your provisional, though?"

"Course I do. I applied for it as soon as I turned seventeen, just never got around to taking lessons." He turns the stereo up to the vampire club song from Blade. "Buckle up, baby. I'm gonna take you for the ride of your life." He chuckles and flashes me a cheeky grin through the rearview mirror. *If only*. My cheeks instantly heat, and I fumble with the seatbelt.

Dean stares at Cal. "You fuck up my car, Cal, I'm gonna fuck up your face."

"Yeah, yeah." He puts his foot on the accelerator and speeds down the street, forcing me back in my seat. He slows down and jerks a little as he gets used to the biting point, then swerves a corner.

"Cal, you're throwing me all over the place here."

He laughs. "Sorry, but that was the idea." He smiles in the mirror again.

"Keep your eyes on the fucking road, dickhead." Dean shouts.

"Okay, keep your hair on." Cal strokes Dean's shaved head. He bats him away and scowls.

I lean over between the two front seats. "Cal, some of us don't have a death wish. Can you just drive sensibly, please?"

He pulls into an empty office car park and speeds up, then pulls the handbrake, sending us into a spin. "How d'you like them doughnuts, Steph?"

I cling on to the seatbelt and giggle.

Dean doesn't look impressed. "All right, you've had your fun. Are we going to get some food or what? I'm starving."

My tummy rumbles at the mention of food. I haven't eaten since lunch. "Me too. There's a Chinese around the corner."

We grab food, picking extra up for Amy, Scott and Jason. Cal calls at the shop for more beers, even though I'm sure the cupboards are full of alcohol as it is. We have more alcohol than food.

Dean gets in the driver's side and adjusts the rearview mirror while Cal is in the off-licence.

I inhale the smell of Chinese food as I hold the bag, heating my lap. "How's the mechanic apprenticeship going?"

"Good, yeah."

Cal gets back in the car and Dean drives us home. The ride is much smoother than when Cal was behind the steering wheel, but he did look hot driving.

After we've eaten, Dean rolls a joint and hands it to me. Cal walks into the kitchen to get more beers from the fridge. Dean sits next to me on the sofa. "What's going on with you and Cal?"

I let out a puff of smoke. "Nothing, what do you mean?"

Dean smiles. "You've not got it on yet, then?"

"We're just friends." I take in another long drag.

"Yeah, right. Why d'you think he dumped Stacey?" He swigs another drink from his bottle of Bud.

I sit up straight, pulling my eyebrows together. My heart jumps up like it's doing the locomotion. "He said he doesn't want a long distance relationship. Has he said something to you?"

"No, but I'm surprised. I thought he would have made a move on you by now. You two are inseparable. I mean, it's fate that you ended up at the same uni."

Cal walks back into the room and hands out beers. Dean looks at me, pressing his lips together with a smile, moving his finger and thumb along his mouth to gesture that his lips are sealed. Cal sits down next to me, wedging me between him and Dean, like a rose between two thorns.

I take another drag of my joint to calm my nerves. Dean gives me a wink. I sink into the sofa, hoping to hide my flushed cheeks. Cal's hand brushes against my thigh, and my heart does a brand new dance. Could he really have finished with her because he wants to be with me?

I LIE in bed thinking of Cal, as I do most nights, drifting off to sleep. Every possible scenario runs through my mind of us getting together; even more now he is single. I still don't understand why he ended things with Stacey, neither does she, but at least she hasn't called me again. My mind wanders as I lie in my single bed and hug my pillow. I imagine his face and hunky nakedness that I regularly see in my dreams.

The door handle clicks, and there's a shuffling sound. I follow the shadow on the floor until Cal comes into view. He walks towards me. I sit up and turn on the bedside lamp to get a better view of his magnificent body. Dressed in black boxers, he's irresistible.

"Are you okay?" I ask, wondering what he's doing here at this late hour.

"No, I'm not all right." The mattress dips when he sits in front of me.

"What's wrong?" I tilt my head to the side, examining his splendid face with his five o'clock shadow, trying to read his eyes that resemble the warmth of a log fire, always giving me that feeling of home. There's no place I'd rather be than cuddled up cosy with him.

"I can't stop thinking about you."

My breath hitches. His hands cup my cheeks as he urges closer to me. Pressing his lips hard against mine, he parts my mouth with his tongue, and I taste the fizzy cola bottle sweets he was chewing on before. I've wanted this for so long. My heart thumps as his hands traverse my body, finding the hem of my pyjama top and then the bare skin of my back. His hot palms against my flesh heat the blood in my veins, and I'm panting between each dart of his tongue.

Our kiss breaks, but only so he can pull my top over my head. He pauses, taking a moment to eye my breasts, licking his lips. His thumb circles my pebbled nipple and my blood sizzles.

"Baby, I'm gonna take care of you."

I suck in a breath. His confidence has me aching for his promises.

"Lie down."

My eyes are wide. His assertive tone makes my walls clench, and I do as he commands.

"I'm gonna make you come," he says, digging his fingers under the elastic of my shorts and I lift my bottom, allowing him to pull them off. "I'm gonna make all your dreams come true, Steph."

I gulp.

Breathing heavily, his eyes rake over my body, running his palms up and down my thighs. "Open your legs for me, baby. Let me see you."

My quivering knees ride up and fall to the side, opening myself up to him fully. He rolls his lip between his teeth, gazing at my pulsing sex, weeping for him.

"Cal." His name is the only word I can utter as he stares for a beat too long.

"Steph." His eyes flick to mine, then back to my throbbing heat that's begging for his touch. His mouth dives between my thighs, kissing my lips there. Sliding his tongue between my folds, he devours me as if licking out a screwball sundae; not leaving a drop of the sweet sauce or cream. My back arches when he reaches my bundle of nerves, sucking as if he has reached the gumball at the bottom of the ice-cream. I fist the sheets, screwing my eyes shut. My body uncontrollably jerks and pulsates like popping candy exploding through my bloodstream, making my toes curl.

Cal lifts his head, watching me catch my breath as I come down from my fizzylicious high.

"I'm going to take care of you like this every day, baby." He slips a finger inside me and my muscles clench around him. "You're mine now, Steph." He works another finger in, fluttering against my tensed wall, and runs circles around my bud with his thumb.

The light bounces off his glistening mouth, drenched in my orgasm. His eyes are as fiery as a volcano ready to erupt; reds and ambers bubble around his pupils, gazing between my panting lips to my breasts that are so hard and pricked up crying out for his attention. He must sense it as he pinches my nipple while his other hand is still flickering inside me and his agile thumb works my bundle of nerves. I moan, calling out his name, and he lets out a groan of his own. His hooded eyes sparkle as if revelling in the pleasure he's giving me.

"Cal. Cal."

"That's it, baby. Scream my name."

The pressure builds in my core.

"That's it, Steph. Come, come again for me." His voice is deep and commanding. "Come now." I do. I come more ferociously than before with a burst of tangfastic pop, crackle and fizz, screaming his name. My mind fills with the brightest of lights, so bright it's blinding and my scream so loud it's deafening. I jolt up in my bed, panting from the overwhelming tingles rushing around my body. The room is dark and empty. I turn the bedside lamp on and realise I'm alone. I flop back on the bed, gasping for breath, with disappointment filling my lungs, hoping I can relive that amazing dream again.

SOON, I'll have enough money to pay Cal back for my share of the house payments with all the extra shifts I've picked up this week. It's the evening now, and customers are sparse. I lean on the front counter next to my till, tapping my blue nails against an empty tray. My mind drifts to Cal, wondering what he's doing now. A hum escapes me as I sigh. I just want to be home. The door opens. A man stomps towards me with an open plastic carton in his hand containing ice cream and what I think is an apple pie. He snarls as he gets closer, then launches the tray at the wall. My head flinches. I hold my breath as the plastic smacks against the tiles.

"Where's the manager?" he growls.

Bugger. Where's Cal when I need him. I pick at my nail varnish. "What's the problem, sir?"

"My apple pie was fucking cold. I want my money back."

The contents of the carton stick to the tiles, but slide down gradually, leaving a smear of ice cream and brown sauce in its wake. What a waste of a good pie.

"Just a moment." I scurry off to find Steve, the manager, who has a permanent smile on his face. "Steve, we have an angry customer. His pie was cold."

Steve gets up from behind the office desk and comes through to the serving area with a smile plastered on his face.

"You can wipe that fucking smile away. You think this is funny, do ya? Do ya?"

It's a good job Cal isn't here. He would have pied this nutjob by now.

"Steph, put another apple pie in the frier for the gentleman."

I nod. Gentleman. He is no gentleman. Although, if his day has been as long and boring as mine, I can sympathise, nothing worse than cold pie.

I get a taxi home after my shift and walk into the house to find everyone here. I grab a bottle of cider from the fridge to unwind. Amy and Scott are in their usual spot on the sofa with their arms draped around each other. Cal is sitting in the chair and Nicola and Jason sit on the floor around the coffee table. The kitchen is full of people with a few others scattered around the house.

A redhead called Bianca perches her pert little arse on the edge of Cal's chair. She takes his joint from his fingers and inhales a small puff. I knew she fancied him. Since he split up with his girlfriend, she's been waiting to make her move. She blows the smoke from her lips and looks at Cal. "Why don't we play spin the bottle?"

He takes the joint back. "I'm not playing that shit."

Amy rolls her eyes. "That's so childish."

Nicola says, "Oh, just because you're all lovey-dovey with Scott. I'm up for it."

Jason agrees, along with a few of the others. "Steph, are you joining in?" Jason asks. They move the coffee table to one side and all sit in a circle.

"Why not?" It's probably the only way I will get any action around here. I'm certainly not going to sit around and watch Bianca slime over Callum all night.

Cal sits on the floor next to me and Bianca's eyes light up. Has he done this for her? I huff. It was bad enough seeing him with Stacey occasionally. God help me if he gets with her, and I have to see them together every bloody day.

I gaze at Cal. "What are you doing?"

"Playing spin the bottle." He grins and stubs his joint out in the ashtray and knocks back a mouthful of vodka.

"But you just said it was lame."

"It is." He chortles, and I shake my head at him.

Bianca starts off with a spin, and I can see her smacking her lips together already. She's trying to land on Callum. I sigh, but the bottle lands on Natalie. Everyone eggs them on. They give each other a cross between a peck and a snog. Next up is Jason. It lands on Nicola. She leans over, all smiles and giggles. Jason cups her cheeks, slipping in his tongue. I don't know where to look, so I glance at Cal. He's watching Jason and Nicola and chuckling to himself, shaking his head. His hair waves around his face. He spots me staring and smiles before giving me a wink that makes me suck in a breath. Daniel is next. The bottle spins and lands on Lindsey. They both give each other a light peck.

It's now my turn. My palms are sweaty. I only agreed to this because Cal wasn't playing. Even though he is the only one here I actually want to kiss, he is also the only one here I don't want to kiss. I know that makes no sense at all and I can't explain it.

I spin the bottle and hold my breath. My heart beats faster with each rotation. It comes to a stop on Jason. I let out a long breath. Jason leans over and kisses my cheek. I'm grateful, but at the same time I feel awkward, like am I that terrible that he can't even bear to kiss me on my lips. Or is it because we're friends? I notice Jason glance at Cal after kissing my cheek, and Cal nods at him. It's his turn next. I can't even look. I contemplate walking to the kitchen to get a drink.

The bottle stops on me. My heart jolts. No. This cannot be happening. As much as I want to kiss him, we can't have our first kiss during a game of spin the bottle. Can we?

CHAPTER

Sixteen

C al turns to me and places both hands firmly on my face, making my breath hitch. I peer into his eyes, unable to read his expression. He seems serious, and I can't stop the giggle that bubbles up. Cal lets go of me and stifles a laugh, dropping his hands to his knees. I look away as my cheeks flush.

"You can't back out now. You have to kiss. Game rules," Jason says.

Cal lifts my chin. "I'm not backing out." He grins and his rough palms rub against the soft skin of my cheek. I smile back as he brings his lips to mine. Our noses touch, and I giggle again.

"What's so funny?"

"You're just so serious."

He lets go of my face and chuckles under his breath.

"Just peck each other and let's move on," Bianca shouts. I wish she would piss off. I want more than a peck. Don't I?

"Okay, okay." I wave my hands in the air and give myself a shake. "I won't laugh this time."

Cal's strong hands tenderly hold my face in place.

His tongue runs along his bottom lip. "I'll show you serious." He tilts my head to the angle he requires. I gaze into his tantalising brown eyes that remind me of fizzy cola bottle sweets, and my mouth waters. I part my lips as he leans closer. Everyone in the room disappears, blurring into a multitude of coloured shapes. His breath falls on my mouth and I get a hint of vodka.

Our lips meet. I close my eyes. They're everything I'd imagined, like a warm sugary doughnut with a runny strawberry centre that sends a burst of excitement down my spine.

His tongue slips through my parted lips, delicately devouring me. My trembling hand rests on his chest. His beating heart matches mine in a fast, pulsing rhythm. The kiss slows, and his grip on my face loosens. I don't want this to end. I could kiss him all night. My hand moves to his neck, so he doesn't pull away, and his unshaven jaw scratches my palm, sending another wave of tingles to my core. My fingers tangle in his hair, falling perfectly around his face. His tongue greedily laps against mine, swirling around his mouth. My thighs clench together as the heat pulses through me. I imagine his tongue elsewhere, aggressively lapping its way around my folds and a soft moan escapes my lips, barely a whisper, but Cal must feel the vibration as his tongue stiffens, and he deepens our kiss in a charge of excitement.

"Ugh, get a room," Bianca shouts. *Jealous cow.*

Cal's mouth widens as he smiles against my lips. He pecks me and pulls away slightly. I open my eyes.

My body trembles with each ragged breath. Everything except him is still a blur as the room spins around me. I focus on Cal's delicious cocoa brown eyes that seem darker now. Rich like my favourite chocolate.

"That was intense," Amy says. Callum removes his hands, and I sense everyone's eyes on us.

"Kate's turn," Bianca shouts.

I stand and stumble into the kitchen with weak legs. My hand shakes as I turn on the tap, and grab a glass from the cupboard. Staring at my reflection in the window, my trembling finger swipes along my lip where his kiss lingers. I can still taste the vodka on his tongue. My palm trails my cheek then my neck where his hand has left tingles still firing there. I can't seem to catch my breath. My head is dizzy, and I'm light as a feather.

"Steph." Cal stands in the kitchen doorway, leaning against the doorjamb with his hands in his pockets. His hair falls in front of his exquisite face as he looks down, kicking at the chipped floor tile.

My mouth can't form a word, let alone a sentence. "Hmm?"

"Are you all right?"

I nod, still dazed and bewildered. I've never felt like this before. My legs are threatening to fail me with every wobble of my knee. I can't speak, barely managing to breathe. My heart had just started to slow down to its normal pace, but now it's speeding up again. I want to go to him, tell him I'm more than all right. I'm on a euphoric plane, and I've never felt more alive. The way he kissed me was everything I've wanted for months. Could he actually feel the same?

"I'm sorry." He glances up at me, pressing his lips together.

What's he sorry for? He's just given me the best kiss of my life, and he's sorry. Did he not enjoy it like I did? Does he not feel what I felt?

How could he not feel the sparks fly through the atmosphere, creating an electrical current that is still present between us and could explode at any moment?

I slump my body against the sink and take a sip of water. "It's fine." Fine? I cringe at my own words. It's more than fine. It was breathtakingly wondrous.

"Are you coming back through?" He nods towards the living room.

"I just need a minute." What I need is to change my knickers, pour liquid down my throat, lie down in a dark room to calm my nerves, and regain some sort of stability.

He turns and walks back into the lounge. I take another drink, but no amount of water can quench my thirst. Should I go back to the party or to my room? I can't watch him kiss someone else like that.

Amy walks into the kitchen. "Steph." Her wide smile and sparkling blue eyes tell me she's feeling everything I am. "That kiss. I've never seen him kiss his girlfriend with that much passion."

"Really?"

"Steph, he obviously has the feels for you, and don't you give me any of that we're just friends bullshit. Friends don't eat each other's faces."

"He said he was sorry." I take another drink of water.

"What for?"

"He just came in and apologised." I wave my hand towards the door where he was standing.

"Why?" Amy's eyes are wide and her hands reach out to touch my arms.

"I don't know. He obviously regrets it."

"Oh, Steph. Talk to him. Tell him how you feel. I know you like him."

"Is it that obvious?" My hand shakes as I lift my glass.

"It is to me, but he's a boy. They haven't a clue."

I place the glass on the worktop and run my fingers through my hair. "I can't tell him how I feel. If he doesn't feel the same, it will ruin our friendship."

Amy holds my arm. "Just talk to him, see if he hints at anything."

"It was just a game, Amy. I'm sure he won't go there with me. He's had plenty of opportunities before to kiss me, and he never has."

"Maybe, but if you don't talk to him, you'll never know."

"Okay." If I'm ever going to talk to him, I think tonight is the night.

I walk through the room. The game continues, but Cal isn't here. "Where's Callum gone?"

Scott points to the ceiling, giving me a wide smile and wiggling his eyebrows.

I make my way up two flights of stairs to the attic room. My skin is coated in a sticky layer of sweat, and my shirt sticks to my back. I don't know if it's the adrenaline or because I'm so unfit. Giving myself a shake, I pat my top lip and run my palm under my fringe to remove the beads of moisture there. I fill my lungs with several long deep breaths as I know when I see him, I won't function.

I turn his doorknob. It's locked. He never locks his door. Does he have someone in here with him? I try to recall seeing Bianca when I walked through the lounge. I turn the knob again, hoping I just hadn't turned it enough the first time, and I hear him growl. "What?"

"I'm sorry." I turn and walk back down the stairs, then hear a click.

"Steph." His gentle voice calls to me.

CHAPTER

Seventeen

H e's topless. His jeans fall deliciously low, and I
notice a dusting of hair below his stomach.

He runs his fingers through his hair. "Sorry, I thought you were someone else."

"How come you locked the door?"

"Er." He shrugs. "I... I didn't want any of them fuckers barging in."

"Bianca?"

He smiles. "Yeah. She's relentless."

He stands sideways and gestures with his hand for me to enter. "Come in."

I walk through and sit on the swivel chair at his desk.

He lies on his bed, resting his hands behind his head. My eyes rake his delicious body. I lick my lips as if gazing at a vanilla slice with custard cream.

"How come you came back to your room?"

He shrugs. "I just wanted to chill." His chest expands and falls with every heavy breath. I scan the room, trying to look anywhere but him as the dampness seeps into my knickers.

"Do you have any snacks in here?" As I say the words, I open his desk drawer where he keeps his stash of crisps and sweets.

"No, don't go in there," he shouts. I pull out an A4 sheet that sits on top of his food. My mouth opens as I examine the creased paper. A naked drawing of me, Kate Winslet style. My round breasts looking fuller and my nipples hard. My plump belly, large thighs and all my naked parts inbetween are on display.

"What's this?" My voice wavers.

Cal sits on the edge of the bed. "I took it off Mark."

"You asked Mark to draw this?" I hold the paper out in front of me, not wanting to look at myself like this.

Cal shakes his head. "No. He drew it. I just took it from him." His voice is calm. He leans closer to me, sliding up to the end of the bed.

"You beat him up, didn't you? Is this why?" I wave the paper in front of him.

"Yeah. So."

"Why would you do that? I really liked him, Cal. Why would you beat him up?" My hands cover my mouth. "Oh my goodness, is that why he ended it with me, because of you? I actually liked him and you ruined it, you bastard." A watery film floods my eyes, making my vision blur.

"Yeah, you would think that wouldn't you." Cal raises his voice slightly. "Go ahead, think the worst of me."

"Well, what else am I supposed to think?"

"Think what you fucking want. Go back to him if

that's what you want." He tilts his head down and looks at his bare feet.

I blink away tears, letting them drip onto my cheek. "I can't believe I sat there crying to you when it was all your fault."

He lifts his head, glaring at me with flared nostrils. "I can't believe you sat for him and let him draw you fucking naked." He waves his hand towards the paper.

"I never did that. I had my underwear on."

His teeth grind together.

"What I want to know is how you ended up with it."

He pulls his hair off his face and fists it at the back of his head. "You think I was gonna let him keep this of you to fucking perv over?"

"So you thought you would keep it and perv over it instead?"

"I haven't been fucking perving over it. Don't flatter yourself."

I wipe my cheek. "So why haven't you destroyed it?"

He snatches it from my hand and tears it in half, then in half again, and lets the pieces fall in front of me. "There." They drift to the floor in pieces, mimicking my broken heart crumbling away piece by piece.

"Stay out of my business in the future." I storm out of his room.

"Don't worry, I will."

He slams the door after me and the tears flow. I run down the stairs into my room and cry into my pillow. I cry for a long time, hoping he will come into my room to apologise and wrap his arms around me. But nobody comes.

———————

I WALK into the kitchen the next day. My eyes still puffy, but I don't care. I want him to know he's hurt me. He's pouring himself a bowl of crunchy nut cornflakes when I walk in. Normally, he would ask me if I want something, but today he ignores me as though I'm a ghost. He takes a spoonful of flakes drenched in milk into his mouth, and doesn't look up from his bowl. I make a coffee in silence, then take it to my room.

I walk to class with Amy.

"What's going on with you and Cal?"

I grip the handle of my bag tight. "He's a dickhead."

"How can you go from that passionate kiss to not speaking?"

"You tell me."

"What happened?"

I sigh as we cross the road, making our way to campus. I tell her everything about the drawing.

"Oh Steph. No wonder you're upset. That's creepy."

"I know, right?"

"But I think it's creepy that Mark drew that. Did you know?"

"No. The picture I saw him draw. I had underwear on, so he must have drawn me again naked. Yes, it's creepy, but maybe he did it because he likes me, but Cal threatened him and beat him up. No wonder he blew me off."

"I'm sorry, Steph, but why do you think Cal did that?"

"I don't know, Amy. You tell me? I will never understand what goes through his head. I mean, it wasn't because he was jealous; he was seeing Stacey at the time."

"Will you talk to him?"

"No, he's seeing that other girl now."

She knocks my arm. "I don't mean Mark, silly. I mean Cal."

"Oh. If he apologises, I'll talk to him."

We arrive in class and, after a few minutes, Cal walks in. He blanks me and doesn't take his usual seat. He sits at the end of the table next to Scott. I rub the ache in my chest and swallow the lump forming in my throat. How can he be so selfish? I'm not backing down. Not this time. He's the one in the wrong.

At break, he disappears. I wait in class as I always do, expecting him to show up with a coffee and a chocolate bar. But he doesn't appear until class starts again, and he resumes his seat next to Scott.

More pieces of my heart break off. I feel betrayed by my best friend. All because he took a dislike to Mark. So what if he ate their cereal or nicked the odd condom or borrowed their stuff? It's no different to living here. Many times I've gone to get something I bought from the fridge and it's gone, or my books have been moved in the living room. If he was jealous, he didn't need to be. I've given him enough signals, and enough opportunities to take things further with me, but despite how much he spouts about how perfect I am, I'm still not good enough for him.

———

CAL AVOIDS ME ALL WEEK. It's our last week of uni before the Christmas holidays. I pick up some extra shifts so I don't have to see him around the house. The silences are deafening when we're together. It's difficult to breathe in his presence through the thick atmosphere.

I walk into the living room around midnight, after my late shift. The smell of weed hits me as I open the door. Everyone is in hanging out. They all must have the munchies as Amy and Scott pounce on me, wondering what leftovers I have in my bag. I pull out a box of nuggets and a large bag of fries that they take into the kitchen to share. I contemplate giving Cal a cheeseburger that I picked up for him. He doesn't move from his chair and doesn't make eye contact. It makes me sad that he doesn't even want to make things right between us. I'm always the one to apologise. Or make the first move, even when I'm not in the wrong. But I can't go on like this. It's tearing me up each time I look at him.

"I got you a cheeseburger." My voice is weak as I hold the wrapped bun in front of me for him to take.

He blows out a slow puff of smoke. "Save it for golden boy."

"What are you talking about?"

"Fucking Picasso. You obviously think the sun shines out of his arse. So go and fucking lick it instead of trying to suck up to me with your lousy cold cheeseburger."

"Cal." I stand in front of him and curl my shoulders inwards.

"What's going on?" Scott says.

Amy walks in with a plate of nuggets and chips. "Here Cal, I plated you up some food."

"I don't want any." He stands from the chair with a scowl on his face like my food is poison.

"Scott, do you want a cheeseburger?" Cal blows smoke in my face. The smell of weed chokes me.

"Thanks, Steph." Scott takes the bun from my hand, and I run upstairs to sob into my pillow. What have I done? Why is he pushing me away? We've fallen out many times before like all friends do, but we've never taken this long to make up.

Amy knocks on my door and walks in. She sits on my bed and hugs me. "I don't get why he's being such an arse. I've told Scott to have a word with him. It's not fair we all have to live together."

I sniffle and wipe my cheeks.

She squeezes my arm. "Come back downstairs, don't stay in your room alone and upset."

"I can't, Amy. I can't take any more of him blanking me."

"Do you want me to bring you a drink or food?"

"No, I'm tired. I'm just going to sleep."

"Dry your tears. He's not worth it."

She closes my bedroom door and goes back downstairs. Minutes later, I hear her shout at Cal.

"What's your fucking problem? She's sobbing her heart out up there because of you."

I don't hear him respond. A few minutes pass, and I hear stomps up the stairs. I hold my breath, thinking he's going to come into my room, but his footsteps continue up the attic staircase. I let out a sigh and close my eyes, wishing for sleep to take me away from here.

THE NEXT DAY I have work again; a morning shift. I come home just after lunch to Scott and Amy smooching on the sofa.

"Hey Steph," she says, pulling herself from Scott's arms.

"Hi, don't mind me." I flop in the chair and kick my shoes off my tired feet, wiggling my toes.

Amy sits on the edge of the sofa. "Scott, you need to tell her what you told me." She nudges him with her elbow.

"What?" I see the sympathetic look on Amy's face and my throat tightens. "What's happened?"

Scott glares at Amy. "Nothing."

Amy stares at him. "Tell her Scott. If you don't, I will."

I sit on the edge of my seat. "Tell me what?"

Amy turns to face me. "You don't know the whole story."

Scott grabs her wrist. "Amy, don't."

"I think she needs to know the truth, Scott." Amy pulls her wrist from Scott's hand.

I clench the arms of the chair. "What's the truth?"

Scott grips Amy's wrist tighter. "Amy, Cal will go fucking ballistic."

"Tell me, please." I glance between the two of them, my breathing heavy and my chest tightening, wondering what's happened. "What's wrong?"

Scott places his head in hands then lifts to look at me and exhales. "Mark showed everyone that drawing of you and told everyone how much of a good shag you were."

Everything stops as I soak up what he said. My stomach roils, and I hold my hands on my belly. I look at Amy. "Is that true?" Hoping she will tell me this is all a sick joke.

She walks over to me and puts her arm around me. "Scott's telling the truth."

"Why do you think Callum beat the shit out of him? Your drawing was circulating around the art department."

My eyes gloss over. "Why didn't he tell me?"

"He didn't want you to know. He said you'd be horrified."

Amy holds me and strokes my arm. "I only found out last night, Steph, or I would have told you."

"Steph, I'm sorry. I wanted to tell you, but Cal warned us lads not to. He said you'd never be able to show your face in that art class again."

Amy hugs me tighter. "Cal didn't want you to know that drawing was all over campus. He thought he was doing the right thing to save you any embarrassment."

"Mark's a fucking bastard." Scott huffs. "He didn't

even try to get the drawing back. That's why Cal beat the shit out of him and for drawing you like that and letting his mates laugh at the picture."

Amy widens her eyes at Scott. "That's enough now, Scott. I think she gets the message."

"You told me to tell her everything. She may as well hear the whole truth."

I wipe my cheeks, needing to see Cal. I can't believe he would keep this from me, but I love him for it.

"Where is he?" My voice quivers.

"He's gone to the train station." Scott says.

"What for?"

"He's going home today for the holidays."

"You might just catch him, Steph. He hasn't been gone long," Amy says.

I slip my shoes back on. "What time is his train?"

"2.15pm, I think."

I look at the clock. It's two minutes past two. The train station is just around the corner. I don't even say bye, I just run as fast as I can—well, it's more of a fast walk—not even a jog. Now is probably the only time I wished I had taken my brother's advice and used the student gym. My black work shoes are not exactly running shoes either, they have a small heel and are friggin' killing my feet after standing in them all morning.

I arrive on the platform and see him standing there. Our eyes meet. I can't stop the tears from falling down my flushed cheeks. "Cal." His name falls from my lips along with a strangled sob

"Hey." He drops his bag and walks towards me, and

I throw my arms around him, inhaling the minty fresh scent on his neck. He hugs me back. "Baby, what's wrong?"

"Why didn't you tell me?" I sniffle into his neck.

"Tell you what?" His arms squeeze my body tighter.

"About Mark... and the drawing. Scott told me everything."

He pulls away to look at me, and his large hands cup my face. "Baby, I'm sorry. I didn't want you feeling worse than you already did."

The tears drip onto my swollen lips. "So you would rather me hate you than hate those jerks?"

His thumb caresses my cheek. "I would rather you hate me than hate yourself."

I move my head slightly and brush my lips against the palm of his hand.

"If you knew what they were sniggering at, you would never have shown your face in that art history class again, and your eyes light up every time a new slide comes on the screen. I didn't want to ruin that for you."

I grip the collar of his leather jacket. "Cal, your friendship means more to me than any slide or class or whatever."

"You will always have my friendship. You would have forgiven me eventually, as you always do."

His train pulls into the station.

"I tried to forgive you last night. That cheeseburger was a peace offering, but you threw it back in my face."

His thumb swipes under my eye, wiping away the fresh tears that fall. "I'm sorry. I'd had a drink, and I was still hurt. You hurt me when you assumed the worst of me."

"I'm sorry, Cal. I shouldn't have jumped to conclusions. Can you forgive me? I know you always have my back." I press my cheek against his neck, and he kisses my hair near my forehead.

"Yeah. Can you forgive me?"

"Yes." I kiss his skin where my lips touch under his ear.

The tannoy sounds, letting us know his train is leaving.

"I have to go." He kisses my cheek. "Have a good Christmas, Steph."

"And you." I sniffle and wipe my nose on my sleeve. He steps onto the train and stands in the doorway. Another train rolls through the station.

"I love you," I say.

"What was that?" He grins.

"I love you," I shout over the noise of the trains.

"Say that again, I didn't quite hear you." He holds his hand to his ear, grinning like a Cheshire cat.

A smile spreads across my face and I shout, "I love you, Cal."

"You'll have to shout it louder. I can't hear with all the noise."

He's laughing as the train rolls out, and I watch him disappear into the distance.

A ping sounds on my phone.

A text from Cal.

I love you, too. Always have.

Enjoyed the book?

Read the rest of the series…
Forever Yours & Forever Mine

Go to the next page to read the first chapter of
Forever Yours.

BOOK 1
THE TEMPTATION SERIES

ANNIE CHARME

PROLOGUE

"You're my best friend, Steph."

"You're mine too, Cal." A lump forms in the back of my throat.

"There's nothing I want more than for us to be together." He pauses and sighs, leaning back against the headboard on his bed. "But if we broke up, our friendship would never be the same."

"I know you're right, but what if we never broke up? Who's to say we'll break up?" I pick at the baby blue nail varnish on my thumb while I swivel from side to side on Cal's desk chair.

"I care about our friendship too much." He tucks his unruly black hair behind his ears.

"I feel the same, but I'm willing to take the risk. Last night was one of the most amazing nights of my life. I don't think we can go back to just being friends after that, do you?"

"You felt it too?" He gazes into my eyes, fiddling with his eyebrow ring.

The stirring returns in my stomach. My body trembles while my mind scrambles to form the right words. His mesmerising dark brown eyes have me at his mercy. "Yes, it was incredible. I want us to be so much more than friends."

"Come here." He holds his arms out, beckoning me over to the bed.

I join him, and he hugs me tight. His warm breath in my hair sends a tingle through my core.

"I just don't want to lose you as a friend." He caresses my cheek with his large hand.

"You won't." My eyes plead with him, hoping he will kiss me again. I lick my dry lips and inch closer.

He tilts his head towards me. "I will, I know I will."

"I promise—if we break up—I'll always be your friend."

He kisses my forehead. "I hope you will. I couldn't bear to not have you in my life."

"Me neither." I sigh and hug him tighter.

"Did you have a good day at work?" He strokes my arm, swathing my skin in a flurry of goosebumps.

"Yes, I actually did." I spent all day reliving the memory of Cal making love to me the night before, our first time together, my best friend. It just sort of happened as we lay on his bed in the attic bedroom of our student accommodation. I look up at him and I want to relive it again. He licks his lips and inches closer, the tips of our noses' gently kiss and our tongues engage in a slow dance once more.

CHAPTER One

"Morning. You must be the new girl."

That voice is familiar.

I drop my warm Danish pastry on my desk like a hot stone and swivel my chair around. He's the last person I expected to see. My mouth falls open, letting the buttery flakes tumble from my lips. The boy I loved is now a man, more delicious than my orange swirl. My taste buds pop like there's exploding candy on my tongue. I could ravish his lips surrounded by the dark scruff on his face. He's smoking hot, but not as hot as my cheeks right now.

His eyes grow wide. "Steph. It's you."

My hand frantically wipes the drool and marmalade from my lips. I close my mouth. My tongue runs along my teeth, removing any remnants of food, while I brush the crumbs from my clothes. My heart does a hop, skip, and jump. *What's he doing here?*

There's an awkward moment where I don't know whether to shake his hand, hug, or ignore him. After all, we haven't spoken in twenty years. He pinches his eyebrow where his piercing used to be. He would always twist the ring when he was nervous.

The erratic rhythm in my chest rings loud in my ears. "Do you work here?"

"Err, no. I thought I would just come and steal some breakfast."

He still has that sarcastic humour, then?

He smiles, running his fingers through his raven hair. "Of course I work here. I'm one of the marketing consultants."

"Oh." I cover my gaping mouth with my hand. This means we'll be working together.

He clears his throat and tucks his wavy hair behind his ear. "I had no idea it was you. I knew a girl was starting today but never imagined..." He pauses.

I've turned into a blob of jelly; it's a good thing I'm sitting down, as I don't think my legs could hold me right now. He continues to gaze upon me, and I gulp the air down my dry throat. There's a jumble of gymnasts cartwheeling in my stomach. After a long silence, I ask, "Where's your desk?"

"It's just here." He gestures to the desk, staggered opposite mine.

"You've got to be kidding me." Did I say that out loud?

"Is that a problem?" He smirks.

"No, no, not at all. I'm surprised to see you, that's all." *Breathe, just keep breathing.*

Finally, a few other people walk in and dissipate the tension. Including my boss, "Ah, Steph. I see you've already met Callum." He waves his hand towards Cal.

"Yes." I don't mention that we already know each other. Cal doesn't mention it either. I let out a breath and relax my shoulders. I'm not ready to get into all that right now.

"Let me introduce you to the team." My boss turns around and gestures to the few people who have just walked in. "This is Chris. He's the marketing specialist."

"Hi." Chris stretches out his hand and greets me with a firm grip. His short hair is going grey on the sides, but it looks good on him.

"And Kelly is our analyst."

She smiles, showing her perfect white teeth, and bobs her head, swishing her silver-blonde hair. I wave my hand at her and mouth the word 'Hi'. She's pretty and looks younger than me, or maybe she doesn't have kids—they certainly age you.

My boss continues to go through the rest of the group. "And James is the promotions manager."

"Hello, Stephanie." James is very dapper in a royal blue suit. Looking much younger than me and fashions the colour well.

"Hello, nice to meet you all." I glance around at everyone and wave my hand in a rainbow.

"There are a few others who will arrive shortly. I'm sure you'll get to know everyone as the weeks' progress."

"Thank you, Sir."

"Call me Jerry." A smile forms under his full grey beard. He's a big fellow with an air of authority about him, but he seems friendly enough—plus, he was more than generous with my salary—I can't ask for more than that. I've been desperate to get another marketing job for a while. My last boss didn't appreciate me, and constantly asked me to work extra hours. I wouldn't mind, but I hadn't had a pay rise in years.

Everyone disperses to the selection of croissants and swirly marmalade things laid out on the table next to the coffee machine. This job is going to do nothing for my waistline. I've never been slim and attend a weekly slimming group just to maintain my current figure; large breasts, curvy hips, chunky thighs, but I can't resist a Danish pastry. I exhale a long breath, relaxing into my chair as I take in my new modern surroundings; an open-plan space with about ten workstations. A smile plays on my lips and I'm filled with a sense of belonging, regardless of Cal's presence.

"Meeting in thirty minutes, folks." Jerry marches through our workspace before disappearing to his private office.

Cal sits down at his desk, which faces mine. Kelly sits next to me on the right. I try not to look over at Cal, but curiosity gets the better of me. Resting my elbows on my desk, I tilt my head in a daze and place my chin in the palm of my hand. He's smarter than I remember. His hand strokes his stubbly jaw and I hear the scratching of a week's growth beneath his fingertips.

My gaze meets with his deep brown eyes and I look away, pressing my mouth together and chewing on my bottom lip. My eyes flit back to his white shirt, a hint of his inked torso peers through the fabric. I try to make out the design on his chest; he didn't have his pecs tattooed when I knew him. I noticed his smart black shoes aren't the usual black boots with large silver buckles he used to wear.

He always wore black. I don't think I ever saw him in anything else. The way those ripped black jeans hugged his toned arse and his black leather jacket hung on his broad shoulders over his Mötley Crüe t-shirt—that's how I remember him. Not that I ever thought of him... much. To survive, I scrubbed away the memory of him until he was nothing but a ghost—now he's back to torment me. My shoulders slump and a wistful smile forms on my face. I'm happy to have a familiar face, but why him? I need to push past this; this job is too good an opportunity to let him mess it up. He already ruined my last year at uni. I'm not letting him ruin any more of my life. For frig's sake, I'm a forty-year-old woman. I need to get a grip.

Cal catches me scrutinising him again and his lips turn upwards in the corner of his mouth, sending a tingle from my head to my toes. I look away, feeling betrayed by my body. How can I react to him this way after all this time?

"Are you ready for the meeting, Steph?" Kelly asks.

I glance at the clock. "Is it that time already?" I've been sitting here staring, not necessarily at him, just staring into space while transported back in time for the last thirty minutes. "Err, yes, what do I need?" Everyone gathers their folders, books and tablets.

"Just a notepad and pen. There are stacks of notebooks in the stationery cupboard if you need one."

She points to the cupboard near the breakfast table, but before I can move, Cal jumps up and grabs a book.

"Here you go." He hands me a notepad. "Do you have a pen?"

"Yes, thank you. Do you?" I smile, remembering how he never carried a pen.

He flashes me an endearing look. "I'm good."

"You can hang your belongings over here." Kelly points to a coat stand behind Cal's seat. "And there's a drawer with a lock and key under your desk if you want to put your bag in there."

"Thanks." I put my things away and follow her to the conference room. We walk past a row of filing cabinets that line the wall to the right. Cal walks to the side of me. I make small talk, not wanting any more awkward silences, but I overdo it with all my questions. "How long have you worked here?"

"About ten years. I had some pretty shitty jobs before that." He lets out a small laugh. "One was working in a sock factory."

"What, making socks?" We studied marketing together, why would he be in a sock factory? We corner the cabinets, and large glass doors come into view, exhibiting a contemporary conference room.

"Nah, it was marketing, but the role was more about creating designs for the socks. You know, those cheesy socks that my mum and Gran would always buy at Christmas."

I let out a laugh that's more of a snort. "Oh those, I remember." I look away. My face flushes, and my hands are clammy. "So, do you live locally?" I ask, trying to recover my mortification.

"Yeah, I live about ten minutes down the road." He opens the door to the conference room and gestures for me to enter. "You?"

"I still live in our hometown." I've always lived there, apart from the years spent at uni. Cal grew up there also—we went to school together—until his mum moved them to the city when we were doing our A-levels. "How did you end up back here, well, in the next town?"

I manoeuvre around the large oval conference table. Cal pulls a chair out for me and takes the next seat. "Long story. I'll tell you about it another time."

"Okay." I want to know more about his life after me. He observes me for a moment, tilting his head as his lips turn upwards. His eyes are the same kind eyes that I remember, crinkling up in the corners as his smile widens.

I smile back, unable to control my reactions around him.

His eyes glance towards my hand that rests on the mahogany table. "You're married." He takes hold of my fingers and touches my wedding band with his thumb. His hand feels rough but warm.

Gazing into his eyes, the gymnasts in my stomach are no longer doing cartwheels; they're somersaulting. How can he still have this effect on me after all this time? I slap myself away from his gaze and look around the room. How dare I let myself feel this way? I hate this boy or man. He broke me; I can't forget that. The room fills and our conversation is no longer private.

"Yes, so." I pull my hand away from his grasp. He was the one I wanted to marry all those years ago. I would have done or gone anywhere with him until he left me stripped of his love. I search his hand for a ring but don't see one.

Jerry walks in to chair the meeting. He starts by discussing a new client; a chain of artisan chocolate stores that want to re-market themselves. This should be good. I can see the diet is definitely out the window now as Sarah walks in with two boxes of chocolates from said company. Everyone dives in, including me, of course. An orange flavour with a crunchy texture makes my mouth water. Next, a zesty lemon with a sugary coating, that tastes just like a lemon meringue. It's clear the packaging and logo are not branded correctly for how luxurious they are.

"Steph, have one of these, they're your favourite." Cal picks a round chocolate from the box and places it in front of my mouth. I automatically bite into it. My body betrays me again, reacting to his as it always would. The caramel centre envelops my tongue and excites my tastebuds, along with the closeness of Callum, my pulse races. The gooey middle drips down my lip. Cal wipes my mouth with his thumb and licks the caramel from his pad. My breathing quickens. I'm high on him and sugar. He slides the box towards me, offering me another, which I can't resist.

Jerry continues to discuss the brand. I re-focus, listen and take notes, expressing my ideas. Everyone seems impressed, including Cal. I've come a long way since we dated, although he helped me a lot through my studies.

We all get assigned our own tasks and I go to my desk to come up with a new corporate identity for the artisan chocolates. I love my job; this is very similar to what I was doing before. I've worked in marketing since leaving university.

Before I know it, it's lunchtime. Kelly asks, "Are you joining us for lunch, Steph? We usually go to the pub across the road."

I had brought my lunch in my bag, but it seems pretty lame to sit here on my own with a salad. "Yes, I'll join you." I grab my jacket off the coat rack and pull out my bag from the drawer, minus the salad.

Cal hangs back for me, holding the door open. I stumble over the threshold; he steadies me, taking hold of my arm, and my face is once again on fire. I'm desperate to make a good impression. Why should I care? I have a wonderful husband at home and two amazing kids—most of the time.

"So, who's the lucky fella?" Cal asks.

"What?" I watch where my other colleagues are walking.

Cal lets go of my arm. "Your husband?"

"Oh, his name is Justin." Everyone crosses the road and I notice a pub on the other side. A large metal swing sign hangs on the wall, displaying the words 'The Black Swan' with an illustration of the same.

"What does Justin do?"

"He's a builder. He runs his family's construction

business. Are you married?" I think I already know the answer to this.

"Nah."

After we parted, I realised he would never settle down. As much as I tried, he had commitment issues. Most likely caused by his parents' failed marriage and his dad leaving when he was young.

We cross the busy road at the pedestrian crossing. "Any kids?" he asks.

"I have one of each, you?"

"Yeah, two daughters."

"Oh." I draw my head back. He obviously stayed with someone long enough to reproduce not one, but two kids. "So, you have a partner?"

"It's complicated, but I'm no longer with the girls' mother."

That isn't a surprise. "I'm sorry."

Cal pulls the door open to the traditional pub and gestures for me to enter. The bar is bustling with people from the industrial estate. Our group commandeers a long wooden table.

"Don't be sorry. She was never the love of my life. Things just happened, and I stayed for my daughter. Then we had Bethy. I stayed as long as I could, but it just didn't work out."

"You still see the kids, though, right?" I ask with bated breath, hoping he hasn't turned into his father after all the conversations he would have with me about rejection.

"Yeah, of course. I get them a few days a week and alternate weekends. They're everything to me."

I smile at him and nod. I can't imagine what it must be like to not live with your children. The thought triggers old memories of loss, stirring up a hollow sensation in my chest that once consumed me. I would no doubt enjoy a break, but not every week. It would kill me not to tuck them in every night. I'm sure I would even miss the constant fighting and bickering.

As I sit at the table, Cal shrugs his coat off and drapes it on the back of a chair opposite me. "What would you like to eat and drink?"

"Can I have fizzy water with a splash of lime, please?" I search for a menu, but can't find one. "Get me whatever you're having." I grab a tenner from my purse, but Cal doesn't take it and walks to the bar.

"Are you all right there, Steph?" Kelly asks.

"Yes, thank you."

"Do you want me to order you anything, I'm going to the bar?"

"Cal is ordering my food, but thank you."

"Is he now?" She glances at Chris and back to me with a smile. "He knows you're married, right? I can't believe he's hitting on you already."

"He isn't hitting on me. Trust me, I would know."

Kelly walks to the bar as Cal returns with my drink and sits down opposite me. "I've ordered you a Brie and cranberry baguette with chips."

"Thank you. How much do I owe you?"

"Nothing, it's fine." He waves his hand in the air to gesture for me to put my money away.

"Cal, you can't go paying for my lunch."

"You get mine tomorrow, then we're even."

"All right, thank you."

Cal picks at the old oak table. "I still can't believe it's you."

"I know, it seems like another life when we last saw each other."

"Yeah, it does. I'm a different person now, Steph."

"Well, you look the same, maybe your clothes are smarter though." A small laugh escapes me.

"Yeah." He titters, looking down at his attire. "I still have my Rob Zombie t-shirts though."

I sip my drink and smile at the memory of me wearing his tops. "So, tell me all about what you've been up to."

"This and that. I lived in Australia for a few years."

"What?" He always talked about travelling, but I always thought he meant for a holiday. I can't believe he actually lived there.

"Yeah, I just packed my bags one day, bought a plane ticket and went travelling. I was only planning on staying till my money ran out, but I ended up getting a job in a bar and staying for several years."

"That's wonderful." My eyes go wide. I sip my drink, trying to quench my unbelievably dry throat. He actually followed his dream of travelling.

"I got a job in marketing out there, eventually."

"What made you come home?"

"My mum was poorly, she had cancer." His tone changes, his eyes gloss over as he talks of his mum. He stares at the table where he's been scratching at a groove in the wood.

"I'm so sorry, Cal." I place my hand on top of his,

knowing how much his mum meant to him and what a lovely woman she was. He turns his hand over and his thumb caresses my skin; the feel of him sends my entire body into mush. Gazing into his sad eyes, I stay silent, not wanting to bring up any more hurtful memories.

After holding my hand for what seems like an eternity, he clears his throat. "She beat it though, eventually. She's a fighter, my mum." A wave of relief washes over me and I let out a breath I didn't realise I was holding.

"I'm so glad, Cal." Tears threaten my eyes.

Kelly returns to her seat next to me and her gaze hovers on Cal, stroking the back of my hand with his thumb. I pull away. She looks at me with her mouth open and then frowns at Cal. My face heats. I tuck my hands under the table, clasp them together, twiddle my thumbs, and chew on the inside of my mouth.

"What did you get up to after uni?" Cal asks, cutting through the thick atmosphere. Kelly turns to talk to Chris and I relax a little.

"Nothing as exciting as travelling. I went home, had a few crappy jobs, dated Justin, and that's about it, really. Quite boring, isn't it?"

"It's not boring. I expected as much. I knew... I hoped you would find someone to make you happy. Are you happy, Steph?" He peers into my eyes. I swallow. Nobody has ever really asked me that before. I mean, really asked am I happy. What more could I ask for? I have a new job, a husband and two children; our family is complete. But after seeing him again, I can't help but feel that something is missing in my life. The hole I've filled since he left me is starting to sag. A black void creeps in where his love once resided.

"Yes, I'm happy."

"I'm glad."

Our food arrives. Cal's burger with chips and my baguette looks delicious.

"Is it all right?" Cal points to my plate.

"Yes, thank you, I can't believe you remembered what I like after all this time."

He smiles before taking a bite of his burger.

Kelly turns to me. She must have cottoned on to our conversation. "Do you two already know each other?"

"Yes," we both reply in unison and tell her we went to school together, nothing more. The situation is bizarre enough without everyone in the office knowing that I loved this boy more than life itself, my best friend, my lover, my man. Except he is none of those things now and he hasn't been for a long time. After getting over the shock of seeing him, spending a morning with him and having lunch together, it's almost like we've never been apart.

My phone buzzes. Oh no, I forgot to text Justin.

"Hi," I say into my handset.

"Hi, how's it going?"

"Everything is going well." I look at Cal and feel awkward talking to my husband in front of him, so I excuse myself from the group and head outside. I've finished my food now, anyhow. "Everyone is really friendly. I had a pub lunch."

"What about the salad I made you?"

I tut. "Well, I wasn't going to sit and eat a salad when everyone else was going to the pub."

"You need to watch what you eat, Steph. Pub lunches won't help with your diet."

My eyes flick upwards, and I grind my teeth. "I'll have a light tea to make up for it."

"Fine, I'll see what's on offer in the supermarket."

"See you later, then."

"See ya."

As I hang up the phone, everyone is making their way outside; it's time to get back to work. The rest of the day goes by quickly. I'm ready for a large glass of wine after the shock of today. I say my goodbyes and wave at Cal as he gets into his black Audi.

By the time I get home, Justin has already started on tea; the smell of chilli fills the entire house. "Did you have a good day?" Justin shouts while I take my jacket and shoes off.

"Yes, it was good." I walk into the kitchen and go straight for the drinks cabinet. "Do you want a glass of wine, Justin?"

He stirs the rice. "Go on then. I'll have the red. There's some low-calorie wine in the pantry for you."

Ugh, I hate that stuff. I sigh and walk into the pantry to get my bottle.

"Are we celebrating your first day?"

"Yes, something like that." I laugh, not telling him the actual truth, that I need something to take the edge off, after being tense all day sat across from my ex-boyfriend. The low-cal white wine tastes refreshing on my tongue at least, but I would have preferred Justin's red. I imagine the rich velvet liquid sliding down my throat.

Just as I sit and relax at the dining room table watching Justin plate up, the kids come running in. "Mum, Cassie called me a stupid idiot," Cairen cries.

Then Cassie follows. "Mum, he was in my room and messing with my dolls." And so it begins. I roll my eyes and take another drink; I have my own problems right now.

"Cairen, stay out of her room, and Cassie, stop calling people names," Justin shouts, seeing my frustration. He places our plates on the table. Cassie has a bigger portion than me.

"Where's the rest of my tea?"

"I've just given you a small amount. You don't want to overdo it after your pub lunch."

I clench my jaw. "Thanks."

"It's made with turkey mince and I've made the sauce myself, so it is slimming for you."

I scowl at him. "So why can't I have a bigger portion?"

"Steph, you know it's not just about what you eat, but also how much. Plus, if you're still hungry after, you can have that salad I made you for lunch."

Even though I'm starving, he's right. He always helps keep me on track.

"So, have you been working on anything exciting?"

"Yes, we're rebranding a chocolate company that

makes artisan chocolates." I tell him about the abundance of Danish pastries in the office this morning, my Brie and cranberry baguette at lunch, and the two boxes of chocolates at the meeting that somehow made their way back to our desks. He doesn't seem impressed and rolls his eyes with each new revelation. "The diet has well and truly gone to pot this week." I laugh. "Hence the wine. I figure I may as well go all in, even if it is only Monday." *Liar,* my subconscious jumps in. *You need the wine to settle your nerves and take your mind off the love of your life.* I sigh. He was the love of my life, but not anymore. *Keep telling yourself that.*

Get the rest of the book
Forever Yours
Available on Amazon and all major bookstores.

Thank you for reading

Lastly, your opinion matters, and reviews make an author's world go round!

Please leave me a review on the following
Amazon
Goodreads
BookBub

Forever Grateful,
Annie

Join my newsletter at www.anniecharme.com

ABOUT
the author

Annie Charme lives in the heart of England with her husband, two children and a randy dog.
She is a graphic artist by day and author by night. When she isn't working, you will find her enjoying time with her family in the English countryside or curled up on the sofa with a coffee, blanket, dog and a steamy book.

Being an avid reader of romance novels, Annie feels that the larger woman is not represented enough, and books about plus size women are very few and far between. This is something that sparked her passion for writing.

www.anniecharme.com

ACKNOWLEDGEMENTS

My husband, you are my best friend. Thank you for all your love and support.

My wonderful, loving parents, thank you for letting me dream and telling me there is no such word as 'can't'.

I am so lucky to have an amazing mother-in-law that shares my passion of books. I am eternally grateful for your love and encouragement.

My friends, thank you for always making me smile.

To my beta readers, I have made friends for life swapping stories with you, and I want to thank each one of you that read and critiqued my work.

ALSO BY ANNIE CHARME

The Temptation Series

Forever Yours

Book 1 of The Temptation Series

Forever Mine

Book 2 of The Temptation Series

Spicy RomCom

When My Ship Comes In

A Naughty Nautical Romance

Unwrapped For You

A Curves For Christmas Novella

Hate Tea Love You

A Man of The Month Club Novella

Romantic Suspense

Protecting Poppy
Taming Violet

Printed in Great Britain
by Amazon